A Real Christmas
This Year

A Real Christmas This Year

by Karen Lynn Williams

Clarion Books
New York

Clarion Books
a Houghton Mifflin Company imprint
215 Park Avenue South, New York, NY 10003
Text copyright © 1995 by Karen Lynn Williams

Text is 12/16-point Sabon.

For information about this and other Houghton Mifflin trade and reference
books and multimedia products, visit The Bookstore at Houghton Mifflin
on the World Wide Web at (http://www.hmco.com/trade/).

Printed in the USA.

Library of Congress Cataloging-in-Publication Data
Williams, Karen Lynn.
    A real Christmas this year / by Karen Lynn Williams.
           p.   cm.
    Summary: Twelve-year-old Megan's efforts to provide a real
Christmas for her multiply handicapped brother and the rest of the family
cause problems with her best friend and some other schoolmates.
    ISBN 0-395-70117-1
    [1. Physically handicapped—Fiction.   2. Mentally handicapped—
Fiction.   3. Christmas—Fiction. 4. Brothers and sisters—Fiction.
5. Schools—Fiction.]   I. Title.
PZ7.W66655Re   1995
[Fic]—dc20   94-43096
                                                     CIP
                                                     AC

BP   10   9   8   7   6   5   4   3   2   1

*To all special needs children everywhere
and their families.
And to Kathy A. and Jackie R.
for their help.*

A Real Christmas
This Year

• chapter 1 •

"Megan!" Amy exclaimed in a whisper. "Did David Morse actually just say hi to you? I know I heard him, but it must have been a mistake, right?"

Megan worked her locker combination and giggled at her friend, who was gazing down the hall at David's back. "Yeah, I guess he did."

"What?" Amy asked. This time it wasn't a whisper.

"Shhh," Megan hissed. "You're embarrassing me."

Amy lowered her voice. "You never told me you know David Morse. He's the cutest boy in the seventh grade. In the whole school." Amy curled herself around her notebooks. "Could you tell if I'm taller than him?"

"I didn't notice. And don't slouch." Megan wasn't sure why, but she felt annoyed.

Amy straightened up. She was tall, and Megan knew she was self-conscious about her height. "Come on, Megan, what's the scoop?"

"No scoop. He's in my English class, but I never talked to him before. His sister goes to Kevin's new school. She's got some kind of mental disability."

Megan's brother went to a special school because he was multiply disabled. Kevin was five but he didn't talk yet, and had only started walking when he was four.

"Wow, I don't believe it," said Amy. "David Morse's sister goes to the Rehabilitation Day School? Why didn't you tell me?"

"No big deal, I guess."

"No big deal? I bet any girl in the school would die if David Morse said hi to her."

"Well, I'm still alive," Megan replied tartly. "Look, Amy, I don't really know him. Besides—" Megan hesitated. "I don't know if he wants everyone to know. About his sister, I mean. He didn't say not to tell, but . . . well, you know."

"Boy, I wish I had a multiply disabled sibling."

Megan groaned. "Don't even joke about it."

"Well, just a little disabled maybe. Anything to get David Morse to talk to me. Being an only isn't so great either, you know."

"Come on," Megan told her friend. "We'll miss the bus. Anyway, we didn't actually talk. We just saw each other there. His sister is cute. She's real petite, chubby with a round face."

"Ugh! You just spoke to the cutest kid in the whole school and all you care about is what his little sister looks like. You're impossible."

"You're the impossible one!" Megan said, laughing in spite of herself. Amy was beautiful, with long dark hair that hung evenly to just below her shoulders. Megan's own hair was all frizz, a nondescript yellow-brown color. Everywhere that Amy was thin and graceful, Megan felt round and awkward.

"What do you mean?" Amy demanded as they left the building.

"I just spoke to the cutest boy in the school and all you can do is slouch."

Amy straightened her shoulders again, blushing. "I am not."

The brisk December air was a relief after the stifling heat from institutional radiators turned up full blast for the winter. Megan took a deep breath and watched with satisfaction as she released it in a frosty billow. "Maybe it will snow for Christmas," she told Amy as they stood shivering, waiting to get on the bus. Amy was coming home with her so they could finish up some Christmas gifts they had been working on since November.

"Maybe," Amy said, but she couldn't be distracted. "He's so cute. Blue eyes with that blond hair, kind of shaggy. Did you notice? It almost hangs in his eyes. And his smile. Shy and beautiful." They found a seat together near the back of the bus. Amy was making dreamy eyes.

"Amy," Megan huffed, "I refuse to talk to you until you talk about something besides David Morse." She turned her back to her friend and sat on the end of the seat with her feet in the aisle.

Megan couldn't be really angry with her boy-crazy friend, even if she tried. Amy was the first real best friend Megan had ever had. They had met at the beginning of the year, when they both had start-ed seventh grade at Torrington Regional Junior High. Megan knew that Amy was as shy as she was and not the kind to get involved with cliquey groups like the one David Morse hung out with. That was one reason they were such good friends. They felt the same about everything. Megan faced forward again.

"You're not really mad, are you?" Amy asked.

Megan shook her head. "Uh-uh."

David wasn't Amy's type. At least Megan didn't think he was. She knew he wasn't her type. Even if he was the cutest boy in the school. He was proba-bly totally conceited.

"Gosh, it's freezing," Amy said as they stepped off the bus. "It would be great if it snowed for the ski trip."

"I hope it snows before that! We still have almost four weeks and I still need a few more baby-sitting jobs." That was the reason they were making the Christmas gifts, to save money. Or at least so Megan could save money. Amy didn't really have to worry about that.

Amy stopped in the middle of the sidewalk. "Megan! You did pay your deposit, didn't you?"

"Deposit? What deposit?" Megan tried to keep a straight face, but she knew she couldn't fool her friend. She had paid fifty dollars from her baby-sitting money way back in October. There was no way she was going to miss this ski trip. Amy already knew how to ski, and Megan had wanted to try ever since she could remember. Dad said skiing was too expensive for a family sport and decent mountains were too far away, so he didn't ski anymore. But now Megan had her own money from baby-sitting and a way to get to the mountains.

"Hey," Amy said. "I bet David Morse skis. I wonder if he's going on the trip."

Megan gave Amy a playful punch in the arm. "Enough about the adorable Morse. Let's go. I'm freezing." She started jogging ahead of her friend. Her backpack bounced, *thump*, *thump*, against her back.

The sweet smell of Christmas baking reached her at the bottom of the steps. It mingled with the fragrance of the evergreen sprigs that decorated the front door. Megan paused on the top step, waiting for Amy to catch up. Suddenly she felt tingly with Christmas excitement, like when she was a kid. She had her hand on the doorknob as she turned back and called to her friend, "Hurry up, slowpoke."

Megan was completely unprepared for the scene that greeted her as she opened the door. Jolted out of her pleasant memories, she stood stock still. A huge roll of wrapping paper was unrolled across the living room like a royal carpet that had been trampled and torn. The floor lamp was tipped over against the arm of the sofa, and the plain white walls were blotched with red and green marker. "Mom?" Megan called.

There was no answer, and Megan focused on the scene in front of her. The coffee table was on its side and a tray of gingersnaps was on the floor, the cookies scattered over the worn shag rug. It was all too familiar but not real. Like a bad dream. This kind of thing didn't happen in their house anymore! Megan wanted to close the door and keep life where it had been a few seconds before. Maybe if she stayed outside in the sharp cold air, this wouldn't be real.

"Let me in. It's freezing out here." Amy squeezed in the door past Megan. "Wow! What happened? Looks like some kind of natural disaster."

"No," Megan sighed. "Man-made." Her barely

audible answer was drowned out as Kevin screamed from somewhere down the hall. How well Megan knew that sound, and still it was alarming. She dropped her books on the couch and ran to the back of the house.

Kevin was in Mom's room. Mom was down on her knees, her body folded around him, rocking gently. Megan had used that same firm restraint and comforting motion many times herself. It came naturally when you lived with a brother like Kevin, or at least like Kevin used to be. But he didn't behave this way anymore. He hadn't for months.

Mom turned toward Megan. As Kevin raised his head, Megan could tell something was different about her brother. But what? His face was thinner or something. In a second she had figured it out. "Mom, what happened? Where's Kevin's glasses and . . ."

"Oh, Megan," Mom began before Megan could finish. "Kevin threw his glasses and hearing aid out the window of the bus on the way home from school. The driver found the glasses, but he couldn't leave all the kids to look for the hearing aid. He told me where it happened. I'd like you to come with me in the car and watch Kevin, so I can look for the hearing aid. I've arranged for Lisa to go home with Rebecca." Megan's sister, Lisa, was in first grade. Rebecca, who lived down the street, was her best friend.

Mom looked past Megan. "Oh, hello, Amy." Her voice was strained. "I forgot you were coming over. I'm afraid we have a change in plans. I need Megan's help."

Megan, too, had forgotten her friend was there. Now she noticed her standing awkwardly in the doorway as Kevin began kicking and thrashing, making his terrible high-pitched scream. Their plans were ruined. Of course she'd have to go with Mom. When Kevin got like this, Mom wouldn't leave him with anyone, and she certainly couldn't leave him alone in the car while she looked for the hearing aid.

Megan moved closer to help her mother, but she hadn't missed the startled expression on Amy's face. Before she could even touch Kevin, he threw back his arm and stuck a finger in her left eye. "Ouch!" she exclaimed. It stung, and Megan felt the tears spring up. She squeezed both eyes tight for a minute until the pain subsided. It wasn't just the pain of a finger in the eye. Her chest felt heavy with disappointment and frustration. How quickly Kevin returned to his old behavior without his hearing aid and glasses!

Mom had Kevin under control again. "Go wait in the living room," she said. "I'll get Kevin's jacket, and we'll be out in a minute."

"Wow," Amy said, following Megan out of the bedroom. "A real one-kid tornado." She managed a false-sounding laugh. Megan knew her friend was trying to joke, but Amy looked shocked. She'd thought Kevin was so cute, but she had never met him BHG—Before Hearing aid and Glasses. Megan could just imagine what she was thinking now.

"I can't believe Kevin could do all this." Amy gazed around the living room.

Megan made an attempt to clean things up. "Kevin's really strong for such a skinny little kid," she said, more to herself. She straightened the lamp and picked up the cookie tray. The mess was hopeless. She sat down stiffly next to Amy. Neither girl spoke, and the silence was uncomfortable. Megan's eyes were watery and her face was hot with embarrassment.

Amy finally said, "I guess I better go home. Maybe I should call my mom." She sounded embarrassed too.

Just then Mom appeared, struggling to confine Kevin in her arms. "I think we can give you a ride if you don't mind going with Kevin," she told Amy. "He likes the car, and he'll probably be all right in his seat."

Kevin was quiet in the car. The motion seemed to relax him. Megan and Amy didn't talk, and Mom drove in silence. Megan could tell she was nervous about finding the hearing aid. The glasses, Mom had shown her, were totally smashed, and who knew what the hearing aid would look like or even if it was still there?

"Thanks for the ride," Amy said when she got out of the car. "See you tomorrow."

Megan just nodded.

• chapter 2 •

Mom glanced at Megan as they backed down Amy's driveway. "I'm sorry your plans have been ruined," she said quietly.

Megan concentrated on looking out the side window. "That's okay," she mumbled. "We can do it another time." But would they? she wondered. Time was running out. Less than two weeks until Christmas. Maybe Amy wouldn't even want to come over again now that she had seen the real Kevin.

But Amy wasn't like that, Megan reassured herself. She was different. That was why Megan liked her so much.

Last year Megan's sixth-grade teacher, Mr. Austin, had warned the class about the difficulties of starting junior high in a big regional school with lots of kids from all over the district: a different teacher for each subject, homework subjects to keep track of, more responsibility. But Megan loved it. It was like getting a new start with new kids—kids who didn't know you had what they called a retard for a brother. You could just get lost in the crowd or try being a whole different person.

It had been scary, but she had met Amy on the first day. They had all but two classes and homeroom together.

The best part was that Amy didn't seem to mind Kevin at all. That was a kind of secret mental scale Megan used to measure people—how they reacted to her younger brother. Amy said it was a life-broadening experience to meet someone like Kevin. Amy was always looking for life-broadening experiences, and she scored high on Megan's judgment scale. Of course, Amy had never known Kevin before this year.

"I think this is the place," Mom said. "The driver mentioned this intersection. He was coming the other way." She slowed down and pulled over. "You just stay here," she added, getting out of the car. "I hope this won't take long."

Kevin had screeched and started kicking as soon as the car stopped. When Mom got out, he began slamming his head against the car seat. Megan reached over and patted him on the arm. "It's okay, Kevin," she said firmly. "I'm still here. Mom is coming back." Megan had twisted herself around with her face squarely in front of Kevin's so he could see her lips. But she felt like she was talking to herself. Out the window she could see Mom still trying to get across the intersection. Sighing, she leaned her head back against her own headrest and closed her eyes.

I'm used to Kevin's behavior, she told herself. *It doesn't bother me anymore.* But she had to squeeze her eyes tightly shut to keep the tears from coming. Why would Kevin do such a thing? He seemed to really like his glasses and hearing aid, and yet once in a while he did something crazy like this. Two weeks ago Megan had caught him trying to flush his glasses down the toilet. Now the glasses were broken and his hearing aid probably lost. He was miserable without them.

Megan knew the glasses and hearing aid were very expensive. They had to be ordered and would take time to replace. Mom and Dad had made that clear many times since Kevin had gotten them.

Mom was back sooner than Megan expected, and for a moment Megan was hopeful.

"I found it," Mom reported. "But it looks like it's been run over." She flipped the switch and turned the two dials. "I can't get any feedback at all. It's broken."

"Maybe it's just the battery," Megan said without really believing it.

Kevin calmed down as soon as Mom started the engine, and he was asleep by the time she turned the car around. Megan felt too tired to say a word. The car ride in the early darkness soothed her, and she let the engine noise and the spaces of dark and light cast by the streetlights wash over her.

They passed house after house decorated with lights for the holiday. This was the first year Kevin had started to appreciate the decorations. He would stare at the tiny bright lights and even giggle and point at the figures of Santa and reindeer. Usually Megan enjoyed the magic too. She knew, each year, which house would have the Nativity, or the huge blue star on the roof, or her favorite, the tiny white lights on each branch of every tree and shrub like a fairyland. She loved them all, those that were tacky and overdone as well as the artistic ones. But tonight, as they drove under the silver garlands that crisscrossed the street in the center of town, all the decorations seemed dingy, fake, and empty.

It was like crossing a time warp, Megan thought grimly. A few short hours ago she had been bubbling with Christmas spirit. This year Mom had been baking and wrapping Christmas gifts. The whole family had been planning a real Christmas. And Kevin with his new hearing aid and glasses was

14

going to make it extra special. Now she was afraid they'd all be transported back to the time BHG.

. . .

Kevin woke up as soon as Mom turned the engine off. He was wild, thrashing and screaming. Mom took him into his bedroom to try and calm him down. Megan could hear Kevin's screeching as she cleaned up the living room and set the table. She looked around to see what she could start for dinner, but she wasn't sure what to do and she felt helpless.

It's a good thing Lisa isn't here, she thought as she slumped down onto the couch. Her younger sister would want all Mom's attention. Right now Megan felt she could use a little comforting herself.

The noise coming from the back of the house told her Mom was still having a rough time in the bedroom. Megan wondered if she should try to help. It was going to be impossible to do homework.

Suddenly she remembered something. The tape player! Why hadn't they thought of it before?

"Mom, Mom," Megan called as she burst into Kevin's bedroom. "Where's the—"

"Megan, please," Mom hissed. She was holding Kevin in her arms, rocking him. He had calmed down, but Megan had been so excited about her idea that she hadn't noticed. When Kevin saw Megan, he started kicking again.

"I almost had him settled." Mom sounded angry. "Close the door and leave us alone."

"But Mom—" Megan started again.

"Megan!" Mom said sternly. "Go."

Megan closed the door quietly, feeling the tears well up again. She wanted to go to her own room and fling herself on her bed and cry all night. Instead, she made her feet carry her back down the hall to the living room. She began searching through the cupboards under the built-in bookcases on either side of the fireplace. Dad had made doors for the bottom shelves so they could have places to keep things away from Kevin. All four cupboards had childproof locks on them. Sometimes Megan had trouble with them herself, especially when she was impatient, like now. She finally got the darn things open and found what she was looking for in the second cupboard. Music tapes. Quickly she flipped through them until she found Dad's tape with "The 1812 Overture" on it.

Back in the kitchen, Megan had to climb up on a chair so she could reach the tape player on top of the refrigerator. It was the only place where the player would fit and where Dad could be sure Kevin wouldn't get to it. Megan carefully took the machine down and stepped off the chair. She popped the tape

16

in and hit REWIND and then STOP and PLAY. Luckily the batteries were good.

"The 1812 Overture" was the first piece on the tape. It began softly. She turned the volume up, hoping Mom could hear it over Kevin's screaming. *Please work,* Megan thought as she carried the player down the hall.

The music was so loud, Megan couldn't hear anything else. Before she reached the bedroom door, it suddenly opened. Mom held Kevin firmly with one hand and waved Megan toward them with the other. As Megan got closer, Mom placed Kevin's hand on the tape player. Immediately the tension seemed to flow out of Kevin's body, and he tried to wrap himself around the black machine.

"Megan, you're a genius. I forgot all about that tape," Mom yelled above the music. She was smiling. "I'm sorry I snapped." She gave Megan a squeeze with her free arm. Together they led Kevin back to the kitchen. Megan put the tape player on the floor next to the refrigerator and Kevin plopped himself down, leaning against the refrigerator with one arm and his head resting on the tape player. He stuck his thumb in his mouth.

The refrigerator was another thing Kevin liked. Mom said it was the warmth and vibration that soothed him. Sometimes he would be leaning against it and suddenly the motor would turn off and Kevin would have a fit, but he hadn't done that for a while. That was another one of those things from the time BHG, which had all seemed so far in the past. Now Megan remembered it had been only a few short months ago.

"Turn it down a little," Mom said as she started getting dinner ready. Megan reached down and turned the left knob very slowly, knowing from experience that turning the volume down too much would set Kevin off again. The doctor said Kevin could hear some without his hearing aid, but Kevin liked the vibrations of the drums and the horns in this piece, and he needed to have it loud enough to drive you crazy if you had to be in the same room.

"Quick," Mom called to Megan, "get ready to rewind." If you caught the overture just as it was about to end, you could rewind it and start it again before Kevin had time to start screaming. "I can't believe we're back to this old game again," Mom sighed as Megan stooped and hit REWIND. Megan knew what she meant.

She straightened up and gazed down at her brother.

Suddenly Kevin looked so cute and helpless that Megan felt an ache in her chest. She just wanted to cuddle him, but she didn't want to take the chance of disturbing the peace and calm. Kevin was such a mystery. If only she could know what he was thinking.

· chapter 3 ·

Kevin had listened to "The 1812 Overture" six times and Megan had just started it again when Dad came in through the back hall. Megan hadn't heard his ride pull up. He stood in the doorway in stocking feet and spattered gray sweatshirt. Dad's latest job was with a masonry crew at a construction site in the next town. Sometimes he even had cement spattered on his face. His face was clean today, but he was frowning when he said, "Sounds like Spiderman has been at it again. What happened?" He raised his voice above the music. "Can't we turn that thing down?"

"Not unless you want to have a one-man tornado on your hands," Megan said grimly.

"I'm lucky Megan remembered that piece, or dinner wouldn't be started yet," Mom said.

"Gee, thanks, Meggy," Dad said, making a face. He was the only one who still called Megan that, but she didn't mind. He smiled and hugged Megan. Then he put an arm around Mom's shoulders. "Looks like a rough day around here. Someone want to tell me about it?"

Mom explained about the hearing aid and glasses. She ended by holding up the bent and twisted glasses and the cracked hearing aid for Dad to examine. Dad waved them away.

He rubbed his forehead and sighed. He was staring at the marker scribbles that extended into the kitchen from the living room. "Oh well, the walls needed a new paint job anyway," he said sarcastically, reaching into the refrigerator for a beer. Megan could appreciate the sarcasm. Dad had painted that wall for the holidays just last month. Before that, all the walls in the house had been marked up and dirty. Since Kevin had gotten his hearing aid and glasses and started school, Mom and Dad had been fixing the house up. The paint job and new curtains were just the beginning.

"It's marker," Mom said loudly above the music. "I'll get it off, Frank. With soap and water." Megan thought she sounded angry, or was it just the way she had to talk above the music? Megan's stomach muscles tightened.

"The 1812 Overture" came to an end with a loud

discharge of drums. Megan hit the rewind switch.

"Try leaving it off," Dad said as he sat heavily in the kitchen chair drinking his beer.

Mom spoke before Megan could hit the stop switch. "I think we better not." She had to yell to be heard above the music, but now Megan was sure she spoke sharply too.

Dad usually took a shower and changed as soon as he got home. Now he just sat there sipping his beer. "Spiderman strikes again," he said.

Spiderman was Dad's nickname for Kevin. When Kevin began to walk, he was all spastic and wiggly. It really did look like he had eight arms and legs. But the name made Megan uncomfortable. She wished Dad wouldn't joke like that. Sometimes it was hard to tell if he was being funny. The way he said it now sounded mean.

Mom stood peeling carrots at the sink. She had her back to them, but Megan could tell she wasn't happy. Megan felt that with each stroke of the peeler something inside Mom was getting tighter and tighter. Sure enough, she turned abruptly and faced Dad. "Frank," she said evenly, "please stop saying that." Then she turned back to her peeling. Dad stared at her back for a minute without speaking.

Suddenly, Kevin got up, walked the few steps to the kitchen table, and stood looking up at Dad. He started rocking back and forth from one foot to the other and moving his mouth in and out, which meant he was grinding his teeth. Dad watched him for a few minutes, looking tired and sad. "The 1812 Overture" was still blaring away.

"Jeez!" Dad exploded suddenly. "Do we really have to listen to that tape again?" He grabbed the newspaper off the counter and left the room. Mom turned and looked at Megan. Megan arched her eyebrows and Mom just shrugged. Kevin started rocking back and forth faster and faster. Twisting his face into a crooked smile, he laughed his "Hee, hee" laugh. Megan was suddenly aware of a throbbing headache.

. . .

Dinner that night was a disaster. Dad said they had to turn the tape off if he was going to eat in the house, and Kevin kept screaming and spitting his food and throwing anything he could get his hands on. He tried to stand up in the high chair, and twice he almost tipped the whole thing over. After the second time, Mom put him down on the floor, and before anyone knew it he had his hands in Megan's plate.

Megan grabbed his wrists and held them firmly. She put her face down in front of his and said loudly, "Stop that, Kevin. I don't like it." Then she let go of his wrists and turned back to her meal. She stared at her plate and pushed her carrots around with her fork. No one was eating much.

Dad broke the silence. "Jim Morgan's out sick. I had to take the bus all the way over to Newington just to get home." Dad had been getting rides to work ever since his truck had broken down early in the fall.

"I'll need the car tomorrow so I can take Kevin's glasses and hearing aid in," Mom told him. "See if I can get them repaired." She got up from the table and put her full plate of food on the counter.

"Sure would like to get that pickup running again," Dad muttered. He still had half of his macaroni and cheese on his plate.

Lisa burst into the kitchen, bringing the cold air with her. Her short black hair stuck up on end, clinging to her purple ski hat as she pulled it off and tossed it on the counter.

"Close the door," Dad growled.

"Lisa, put your hat in the hall," Mom said wearily.

But Lisa just stood in the open door and made a face. "That's disgusting," she squealed, pointing at the table. Kevin had reached up and was squishing Dad's macaroni in his fist.

Dad grabbed Kevin by the wrist and tried to wipe his hand with a napkin. Kevin shrieked and pulled away, shaking food all over the kitchen. Dad jumped back to escape the spray, and his whole plate went on the floor.

"That does it." Dad threw his napkin on the table and walked out of the room.

"Boy, am I glad I got to eat at Rebecca's," Lisa said.

Mom looked as if she were going to cry, and Megan got up to clear the table. "You should have stayed there," she said under her breath.

. . .

Amy called after supper. "Hi! I get to take a break from tree decorating while my mom looks for the tinsel. How's Kevin and what's all the racket?" "The 1812 Overture" was blaring away again in the kitchen.

Megan squeezed herself deeper into the coat closet in the living room so she could close the door. She explained about Kevin and his favorite music. "He likes the vibration when the cannons go off."

"That's pretty funny," Amy said.

Megan was about to tell her it wasn't funny at all, but she caught herself. She was glad Amy had called.

"Well, here we're listening to 'I'm Dreaming of a White Christmas,'" Amy chattered on. "It's some famous old singer my father likes. I'm about to get a lecture on hanging the tinsel straight up and down with only one piece on each branch. Guess I'd better go. See ya tomorrow."

Megan hung up wishing someone was about to give her a lecture on tinsel and that they were listening to "I'm Dreaming of a White Christmas." Too bad Kevin didn't find Christmas carols soothing, but then, Megan thought as she heard the drums in the next room, she'd probably hate listening to them that loud.

Luckily Megan didn't have much homework, and she finished quickly. Lisa was already asleep in the other twin bed in the room they shared. In the small circle of light from her desk lamp, Megan examined the Christmas gifts she and Amy had been working on.

They had started weeks ago. First they made fabric-covered-bead necklaces for their favorite teachers and one each for their mothers. The necklaces had been Megan's idea, and Amy said they looked really professional.

Mom had helped them with the paperweights, which they made from Kevin's baby-food jars. Megan had made one for Lisa. She glanced across the room to make sure her sister was still asleep before taking the paperweight out of the shoe box where it had been hidden. It had a tiny plastic angel inside, standing in snow with silver glitter and a few glitter stars floating in the water around her. Megan shook the jar and watched the glitter and stars swirl and sparkle and settle again, creating a tiny magical world that almost came alive.

Megan sighed. All the Christmas magic in their house had gone out the bus window with Kevin's hearing aid and glasses. The glitter had stopped swirling in the paperweight, leaving just a baby-food jar and a cheap plastic angel.

It had been quiet for a while as Megan headed for the bathroom to undress for bed. But then Kevin began wailing in his room. "The 1812 Overture" started up. Again! It was still playing when Megan went out to the living room to say good night to Mom and Dad. Lisa came stumbling down the hall behind her.

"It's too loud," Lisa said, looking sleepy. "It woke me up and I can't get back to sleep." The whine irritated Megan. Lisa had her thumb in her mouth, something she hadn't done since BHG. "I can't sleep."

"What's the matter?" Dad asked. "Spiderman giving you nightmares?"

Lisa took her thumb out of her mouth long enough to giggle and say, "Spiderman. Daddy, that's silly."

Dad tousled Lisa's short black curls. "At least someone appreciates my jokes."

Mom scowled and Megan thought she looked

like she was going to lose it. Megan took Lisa's hand and said, "Come on. I'll read a story. 'Night, Mom, 'night, Dad."

Lisa dragged behind Megan, but at least she came. "I can't sleep," she whined stubbornly.

Couldn't have tried very hard, Megan wanted to say. Instead she said, "Come on, Lisa. Give Mom and Dad a break. They've got lots of problems with Kevin now."

"I don't care."

Megan sighed. She was tired too. "Look, if I read you some stories from your Christmas book, will you go to bed?"

Lisa nodded, her thumb back in her mouth. Megan sat on the bed and began reading "The Night Before Christmas." Lisa was asleep before Megan had finished the second story, and Megan tiptoed to her own bed.

The house was quiet again, and Megan let herself relax and snuggle under the covers, little by little trusting the peace that finally seemed to settle around her.

Later that night, Megan came awake slowly from a deep sleep. She could hear voices and realized it was Mom and Dad. There was another sound too, a strange nasal wailing sound. Kevin!

"I've got to get some sleep," she heard Dad say in a muffled voice. Megan listened drowsily to foot-

27

steps and creaking doors. She caught phrases as her parents went down the hall to Kevin's room: "Should have known." "Even with the hearing aid." "A mistake." That was Mom, Megan thought as she began to doze off again.

Suddenly the word "institution" thundered through her half sleep, even though it was in a muffled tone like all the rest.

"Better than this." Dad was speaking now, and Megan was alert, holding her breath, straining to hear.

But Mom didn't reply, or they had gone back to their room.

Megan continued to take shallow breaths and listen, but all she could hear was the rushing in her ears.

She lay wide awake now. Could Mom and Dad have been talking about sending Kevin away? Megan tried to remember what she'd heard. She couldn't be sure, but that must have been it. *How could they?* Megan thought. Kevin had been without his hearing aid for only one day, for Pete's sake. He'd get his aid and glasses back as soon as Mom could take them to be repaired. Sending him away was one of the things Mom and Dad used to argue about BHG. They didn't have fights, just angry silences that made Megan's stomach twist into knots the way it was twisting now. It seemed like

Dad wanted to look at places to send Kevin but Mom wouldn't talk about it. Megan had always been afraid to ask because she didn't want to cause an explosion.

Sometimes she played with the idea that maybe she wanted Kevin to be sent away. But Kevin would never understand if one day they just left him somewhere strange. That's as far as Megan ever got: a picture in her mind of leaving Kevin alone with strangers without any way to explain to him . . .

Megan tried to calm herself. Maybe she'd made a mistake. Now that the word had stopped ringing in her ears, she couldn't be sure she'd even heard correctly. She hadn't heard anything that sounded like real fighting.

Megan had stopped straining to listen. She took a deep breath and began to relax again. They couldn't send Kevin away at Christmas. This was going to be his first Christmas with his hearing aid and glasses. Mom would get them repaired. They were going to have a real Christmas this year, Megan told herself. She looked over at her sleeping sister, almost wishing Lisa would wake up. She would get into bed with her then, like she did when Lisa used to have nightmares, and feel close and peaceful. But Lisa's breathing remained soft and even, and it was a long time before Megan got to sleep again.

· chapter 4 ·

"I hate oatmeal." Lisa pouted and folded her arms across her chest. "Why can't we have cornflakes?"

"The cornflakes are all gone," Mom said wearily as she tried to guide a spoonful of the gooey gray cereal into Kevin's mouth. Megan had to agree that watching Kevin eat didn't exactly make the oatmeal appetizing. Kevin already had it smeared on his face and in his hair, and there was a tiny blob on the tip of his nose. Even so, Megan thought he looked a bit like an elf, a Christmas elf.

Unfortunately there wasn't much Christmas spirit in their house this morning. Dad had left before anyone was up. Mom's hair wasn't even combed, and Megan was surprised to see how gray it looked. She'd always thought her mother's hair was the same yellow-brown color as her own.

Lisa was being especially difficult. After breakfast she demanded that someone help her find her shoes instead of looking for them herself. When Megan offered to brush her hair, she said, "I want Mommy to do it," and kept wiggling and pulling away when Megan tried to brush. Megan lost her patience and yanked at her sister's hair.

"Ow!" Lisa yelled.

"Listen," Megan said, raising her voice, "you aren't the only person in this house."

"And you aren't my boss," Lisa shouted back. She stuck her thumb in her mouth and glared as though she were casting an evil spell on Megan.

"Mom and Dad have real problems," Megan whispered angrily at her sister. "Don't you even care? I heard them talking last night. Do you want . . ." Megan stopped.

"Want what?" Lisa asked.

Want what? Lisa's question echoed in Megan's mind. Want Kevin to go away to a school? Want Mom and Dad to get a divorce? None of that was going to happen. There was no point getting Lisa all upset.

Megan sighed. "I don't know, Lisa. Look, do you want Christmas to be spoiled? Remember all our plans? Kevin broke his hearing aid and glasses. We all have to help."

"It's all Spiderman's fault." Lisa used Kevin's nickname like it was a bad word. "I wish we could send him away like Rebecca's mom said."

"What did Rebecca's mother say about Kevin?" Megan felt her heart begin to pound.

"She said if he went away, Mom wouldn't have so much trouble."

Megan's hand holding the hairbrush fell to her side. Why was everyone talking about sending Kevin away all of a sudden?

"She doesn't know anything about it," Megan said, getting angry again. "You don't really want Kevin to go away."

"Yes, I do. He's a pain. An ugly Spiderman."

"Don't say that, and don't call Kevin Spiderman," Megan scolded.

"That's what Daddy calls him," Lisa said, grabbing her backpack off her bed. Megan took one more swipe at Lisa's hair with the brush, but her sister dodged past her and down the hall.

Megan turned to the mirror to tackle her own hair, wishing briefly that it were smooth and shiny like Lisa's. No use trying to get it to lie flat. She glanced at the clock. She'd be lucky to make the bus as it was.

. . .

Amy was waiting at Megan's locker. "Hey," she said as soon as she saw Megan. She was smiling and her face was flushed. "You're late. Look, I brought you an ornament for your locker. Hurry and open up. I feel dumb walking around with this thing."

"Gee, thanks." Megan stuffed her bulky ski jacket into the locker and took the shiny silver bell from Amy. She hung it on the hook in the middle of her locker.

Amy's excitement was catching, and Megan forgot how tired she had been after a bad night's sleep. "What did you do? Undecorate your tree?" she joked.

"We have so many ornaments, we can't fit them all on the tree. No one is going to miss one little bell. How's Kevin doing? 'The 1812 Overture' didn't blast away all night, did it?"

"Dad made us turn it off some of the time. Kevin's still pretty wild." Megan told Amy about how awful dinner had been and about how Kevin was awake during the night.

"Gosh, my parents would go ape if someone started throwing macaroni and cheese around our kitchen," Amy said. "My mother gets crazy if I drop a crumb."

Megan couldn't picture Amy's parents arguing with each other in the middle of the night either. She didn't say anything to her friend about what she'd heard. Or thought she'd heard, she reminded herself. Somehow, in the daylight, away from home with a friend to talk to, things didn't seem so bad.

Last night really was like a bad dream, and Megan wanted to keep it that way. "My Dad keeps saying things like 'the return of Spiderman,'" she told Amy.

Amy giggled. "Why does he say that?"

"That's what we used to call Kevin before he got his hearing aid and glasses."

"BHG," Amy said.

"Right."

"I wish my dad said funny things sometimes."

Megan could picture Amy's dad in his business suit and tie and the hat he always wore. Amy said he was almost bald. "Sometimes my dad doesn't seem so funny," Megan mumbled. Amy just wouldn't understand. She sighed and changed the subject. "So how's the tree?"

"Great, I guess. It looks the same every year. Just the right shape, not too much off the top, best side out, a star on top. The littlest ornaments are all near the top and big ones near the bottom." Amy made her voice sound like a robot. "Tinsel, one strand on each branch, hung perfectly evenly, straight up and down."

It was Megan's turn to giggle. "You make it sound awful."

"No," Amy said, "it's perfect. That's the problem—too perfect." Suddenly she brightened. "So when do you go to pick up Kevin next?"

"For Pete's sake, Amy! Kevin may not be able to

go to school without his hearing aid and glasses. You saw how he was." Megan knew that the school had only taken Kevin on a kind of probation. It really wasn't a place for someone like Kevin. The problem was, Kevin didn't fit in anywhere.

"Okay, okay. Are you still coming with me to get my hair cut after school?"

Megan knew Amy would be upset. She looked at the floor. "I can't. I have to baby-sit."

"Megan, you promised."

"Mom needs me so she can do some Christmas stuff. She said she'd pay me this time, and I need the money. I'm sorry."

"You always have to baby-sit," Amy said accusingly.

"I need the money for the ski trip."

The bell rang. "Gotta go," Amy said.

"See ya later," Megan called after her friend, but she knew Amy hadn't heard.

. . .

Megan followed Amy through the crowded cafeteria, juggling her tray and notebook and wishing she'd had time to go to her locker before lunch. "Why are we sitting here?" she asked, putting her tray down next to Amy's. They always sat in the same place, if they could get it, two seats at the end of the table in the corner by the window. Today, Amy had picked two seats almost in the middle of the cafeteria at the end of a table full of eighth graders.

"Look who's sitting two tables away, behind you," Amy said in a low voice.

Megan turned around and saw a bunch of kids whom she recognized as seventh-grade student council members. Kristen Webb, Scott Wood, a couple whose names she didn't know. David Morse was there too.

"Oh, I get it." Megan rolled her eyes and pulled out her chair. "Mr. Dreamboat is over there." She sat down across from Amy.

Amy was craning her neck to see around Megan. "What's he eating? Could you tell?"

"Amy," Megan moaned, "are you serious?"

She was relieved when her friend grinned. "Just kidding."

Megan poked at her sloppy joe. It had the same smell as everything else they served in the cafeteria, kind of metallic and sweet. She'd have to ask Mom to get some lunch food so she could pack her own. It would take longer in the morning, but it would be cheaper, and she needed every cent for the ski trip.

"I can't believe we got these seats," Amy said. "Hurry up and finish. Maybe you could say hello to David when we put our trays back."

"I can't believe we're sitting here when our two

36

regular seats by the window are empty," Megan said. She was getting a headache. It seemed like everyone in the whole room was yelling and screaming. "Let's hurry up so we can get out of here. I have to go to my locker before next period."

"Come on, Megan. Just say hello. It would only take a minute. I was talking to Kristen this morning, and she says David is kind of shy."

"Kristen Webb?" Megan asked. "Since when are you two such good buddies?"

"I hardly know her, but she's in my gym class." Gym was one of the two classes that Megan didn't have with Amy. "She's good friends with David. They've known each other since kindergarten. She says David is smart and he's very protective of his sister and the family calls her Rosebud." Amy stopped to take a breath.

"Well, I bet he's a real jerk," Megan said. She didn't mean to sound so angry, but her head hurt and lunch was terrible and she wished Amy could talk about something besides David Morse and Kristen Webb.

"How do you know he's a jerk? Kristen says he's real good at basketball, which is unusual because he's not all that tall. Although he's not short," Amy was quick to add. Megan noticed she was slouching again. "He wants to be a physical therapist someday. Isn't that great?"

Megan ignored her friend's enthusiastic comments. "I know he's a jerk," she said, "because he hangs out with Scott Wood, who is definitely a jerk. Scott went to Beechwood Elementary School, and his idea of funny is telling retard jokes in the back of the class when the teacher can't hear. One day my mom came to pick me up with Kevin in the car. After that, Scott used to make crossed eyes at me all the time."

"Well, maybe you're right, but that doesn't mean David is a jerk. Kristen seems pretty nice, and she thinks he's okay."

"Right, Amy. She's Miss Popularity. All those kids hang out together. Probably they're all stuck-up too. If you know Kristen so well, why don't you go say hello yourself?"

"Gosh, what's your problem?"

Megan didn't answer. She concentrated on opening the tab on her vanilla pudding cup even though she didn't feel like eating dessert. She supposed she should be glad Amy didn't seem to be angry about this afternoon.

"Anyway," Amy added, "they're leaving, so it's too late to go over there now."

Megan watched over her shoulder as David stood and twisted his brown lunch bag into a tight ball. He jumped and tossed it easily over a whole row of tables toward the six huge trash cans against the kitchen wall. Scott made a false lunge at David as if to stop his pass, and the two boys pretended to wrestle in the aisle, exchanging fake blows.

Mrs. Edwards, the lunch aide, scurried toward them, blowing the whistle around her neck. "Move along, boys," she said with a frown, and the whole group from the table shuffled toward the door.

"Pretty juvenile," Megan muttered as she turned back toward Amy.

"He blushed," Amy whispered. She was busy cleaning up her tray as the group of kids approached.

They all passed by without seeming to notice Megan and Amy except for Kristen, who made a little waving gesture and said, "Hi, Amy."

Megan was relieved she hadn't stopped to talk.

"I guess we can go now." Amy stood abruptly, pushing back her chair and picking up her tray.

Megan stood up, finished the last gulp of milk in her carton, tucked the straw inside, and went to empty her tray. She met Amy outside the cafeteria door. "I've got to go to my locker."

"Me too," Amy said as she turned toward the stairwell to the second floor and her locker. She pushed the door open and paused. "Sure you can't come with me after school?"

"I told you," Megan said. "I have to baby-sit."

"I know," Amy said with resignation, and the heavy door swooshed shut behind her.

• chapter 5 •

When Megan got home, Mom had Kevin tied into his high chair with a torn-up old sheet. He looked as though he was wearing a large bandage around his middle. It reminded Megan of when Kevin was in the hospital. He had had fifteen operations before he was four years old. Practically his entire insides had to be remade. He had looked like a little mummy all bandaged up.

Poor Kevin had had a hole through his nose and the roof of his mouth. That was why he still hadn't learned to talk. The doctor said he was going to need more operations on his palate. No one knew how much Kevin could see or hear even with his glasses and hearing aid. His teacher said Kevin's development was delayed partly because of all the time he'd spent in hospitals getting what Megan's dad called his repairs.

Once Megan had heard Aunt Martha say Kevin was a mistake that should have never happened and that he should be in an institution. Mom got real mad and made Aunt Martha leave, and then she cried for most of the afternoon. Megan could still hear those words, and they still made her whole body tighten up.

Little kids and even some adults were afraid of Kevin, but Megan liked his stick-up hair and big ears. She thought he was even cuter when he got the big, thick glasses that emphasized his crossed eyes.

Kevin made his usual nasal snorting sounds— "Na, na, na"—when he saw Megan. Things seemed calmer than they had been yesterday. No "1812 Overture" blasting away, and Mom had washed the marker off the walls.

"Any news about Kevin's hearing aid and glasses?" Megan asked hopefully.

"Mr. Johnson wants to see them. I'm going to take them in now." Mom was already wearing her coat. "I think he'll be okay here with you. He's much calmer today. Call Mr. Johnson's office if you have trouble. I won't be long." Mom was standing in the entrance to the living room, behind Kevin, and he didn't even notice that she was speaking.

"We'll be fine," Megan told Mom as she went

out the door. She offered her brother a graham cracker to distract him. "Glad to see you're feeling happier today," she said as he took the cookie and screeched with excitement. He held it up to his face as if examining it and then held it straight out in front of himself, his arms and whole body rigid with delight. Smiling his crooked smile again, Kevin threw his head back against the high chair and smashed the cookie on the tray.

He sat motionless, looking at what he had done, then suddenly began rocking from side to side. His high-pitched wail startled Megan even though she had been looking right at him. Megan knew all Kevin's sounds, and she knew this was his angry sound. Kevin shook his head furiously from side to side and pushed the smashed graham cracker onto the floor.

"It's okay, Kevin." Megan quickly handed him a new cracker. "Now don't smash it," she said.

Kevin smiled. This time he put one corner of the cracker in his mouth and smacked it with his lips, making humming noises at the same time. Happy sounds.

"That's the boy," Megan said as she ruffled Kevin's straight red-brown hair. He already had gooey mashed graham cracker all over his face. Megan found a place that wasn't too yucky and kissed him on the cheek.

Maybe things weren't going to be so bad after all. Megan stooped to pick up the broken cookie. Maybe they wouldn't have to go all the way back to BHG. Maybe Christmas would be okay, and maybe her surprise plan for Mom and Dad would still work. "Come on, Kevin. We have work to do."

She got a cloth and placed one hand on Kevin's head. He even had graham cracker mush in his hair. "Come on, you little piggy," she coaxed him as he wriggled and squirmed, dodging the washcloth. Kevin was always drooling, and his nose always ran, so wiping his face was a gross job. Megan gave up. "Okay, be a piggy if you want to," she told her brother as she untied him. She was careful to hold him firmly by the arm as she set him down on the floor and guided him directly to his room.

They both sat down on the mattress on the floor where Kevin slept. It was safer than a bed, and it was the only furniture in the room. His stuffed animals and puzzles and books were strewn all over the floor.

It was lucky that Lisa had a Brownie meeting and was getting a ride home with Rebecca's mom, Megan thought, so she could have some time to work with Kevin. She found the worn copy of the farm-animal book on the floor under the pile of bed sheets and quilt. The cover had been torn off and the pages were frayed. "Come on, Kevin. Let's do some animal sounds."

Kevin had stood up with his back to her and was staring down at his ragged stuffed dog, rocking from one foot to the other. Megan got up, took him by the arm, and gently led him back to the mattress. She sat down next to him, making sure she was facing him with her lips at his eye level. She held the picture of the pig up close to her face so Kevin could see the book and her lips at the same time. "Oink, oink," she said. "Pig. Oink, oink." Pig was Kevin's favorite picture. "Come on, Kevin. Oink, oink. Say it."

They were working on animal sounds in Kevin's new school, and the speech therapist had told Mom to work on them at home. Megan was helping. A few weeks before, Kevin had run to Megan with the animal book and pointed to the pig picture. Now they always had to start with that picture. Kevin liked the *Three Little Pigs* book too. It had been exciting to realize that Kevin knew the pictures were different. That was when Megan had gotten her idea about the surprise.

She was working with Kevin on animal sounds every chance she got. It was supposed to be a surprise for Mom and Dad. After all the gifts were opened on Christmas morning, she would nonchalantly say, "I almost forgot, Kevin and I have a special gift for everyone." Then she would get the animal pictures out. Or maybe have the book wrapped. She didn't have anything else for her parents to open except the homemade necklace for

Mom. Mom and Dad could unwrap the book, and then Megan would hold each picture up and Kevin would make the appropriate sounds. It was going to be the best Christmas gift ever.

There was only one problem. They had been working on it for weeks, but Kevin still didn't make one sound. And now he didn't seem to be interested. He wouldn't even look at the book. Megan tried to turn his head toward her, but he started making his screeching noise and shaking his head in short jerks from side to side. He batted the book right out of Megan's hand.

"Kevin," Megan said angrily, "stop it." She grabbed him by the head with both hands and made him look straight at her with her face right down in front of his, so close she could feel his stale breath. "Stop it. Don't you want to learn how to talk?" In a flash Kevin was up off the mattress throwing books, stuffed animals, and puzzle pieces around the room. At the same time he was kicking and screeching, and his hair flew around as he shook his head violently from side to side.

"Kevin, Kevin." Megan tried to soothe her brother, but he pulled away from her grasp.

"Mommmm, Mommmm!" Lisa burst into the room with her hands over her ears, stopping short when she saw Megan. "Where's Mom?" she demanded. She covered her ears again. "Make him stop."

"Mom's doing errands and—" Megan yelled at her sister, then stopped when she realized Kevin had stopped his screaming. Now he was staring at Lisa and rocking back and forth from one foot to the other.

"I forgot," Lisa said as she disappeared out the door.

Megan sighed and closed the door behind her sister. She started picking up the mess. It was useless to try to work with Kevin without his glasses and hearing aid. He was in the corner of the room now, with his back to her, rocking from side to side. She sighed, wondering if he knew he didn't fit in anywhere. Sometimes Megan thought she didn't fit in either. Today she had a scary feeling that maybe she didn't even fit in with Amy, but she tucked that thought away before it could become too real.

Suddenly Lisa was back. Her coat was off and she had a notebook and pencil. "Megan," she said, bouncing down on Kevin's mattress, "I'm making a list for Santa. I'm getting a Ginny doll just like Rebecca's and a real little stove that cooks real food like cupcakes and stuff. Annnnd . . ." She stopped for a breath. "I'm going to get real pierced earrings."

"You don't even have pierced ears," Megan reminded her sister.

"I know, but when Santa brings the earrings, Mom will have to let me get them pierced."

"Just don't be disappointed if Santa doesn't come through with that request," Megan warned her sister.

"He will too," Lisa said. "Santa is magic. How do you spell *pierced*?"

Megan spelled while Lisa added her request in big uneven letters.

"Mom told me how to spell the other stuff, but I don't want her to know about the earrings. So what are you getting for Christmas? Want me to make a list for you?"

"I'm too old for Santa," Megan said, flopping down on her stomach next to Lisa. She propped herself up on her elbows and rested her chin on her hands.

"How can anyone be too old for Santa? I told you he's magic."

"He doesn't bring Mom and Dad anything, does he?"

Lisa had to think about it for a minute. "Well," she finally said, "I won't be too old when I'm twelve." She folded her arms across her chest and glared at her sister. Kevin came back to the mattress and stood over the girls, staring down at them, his head tilted sideways so he could see them right side up.

Lisa giggled. "Kevin, you're funny."

Megan rolled over and closed her eyes. She was

glad Lisa still believed in Santa Claus. Things like Christmas lost some of their excitement when you got older. Megan just didn't feel the same way Lisa did about some things. Sometimes it made her sad, but this year was supposed to be different. Kevin had his hearing aid. It was his first real Christmas and, in a way, Lisa's too. This year Mom had time to make cookies now that Kevin was in school. She was even thinking about getting a job so they could afford more stuff. Dad said that since Kevin was a little more "user friendly," they could get a real tree this year, not just use their tiny fake one.

Megan could remember back before Kevin, when Mom used to sew her a new Christmas dress every year and Dad used to sing Christmas carols in the shower. But Lisa didn't remember before Kevin, and things were different now.

Kevin! Megan sat up. "Lisa, where's Kevin?" Before her sister could answer, she was up off the mattress. "Lisa, you left the door open." Megan flew down the hall. Kevin wasn't in the living room. It had been only a minute or two since Lisa had come into the room. He couldn't have vanished, for Pete's sake! Megan's stomach was in knots.

Kevin was not in the kitchen. Megan checked the back door. At least Lisa had locked it. "Kevin," she called again as she headed toward the living room and the front door. How could someone so uncoordinated move so fast? She had just closed her eyes for a minute!

The front door was locked too, so he had to be somewhere in the house. Megan headed back toward her own room. "Kevin, where are you?" This was all Lisa's fault. She should have closed the stupid door! Megan's heart was pounding. She'd gotten out of the habit of watching Kevin closely since he'd gotten his hearing aid.

A quick glance showed her he wasn't in her bedroom.

"Hey, Megan." Lisa's voice came from the bathroom. "He's in here."

"Kevin!" Megan exploded when she saw her brother. She felt shaky with relief. Tears sprang to her eyes.

Kevin was sitting on the floor on the other side of the toilet with gobs of toilet paper unraveled around him. The whole roll. "Kevin, what did you do?" Her brother ignored her, kicking at the soft folds of tissue draped in heaps across his legs.

"Lisa, this is your fault. You have to clean it up."

"I do not," Lisa shouted.

Kevin looked up over his shoulder, squinting through one half opened eye. He looked back at the paper on the floor and giggled.

Lisa started to laugh. Kevin clapped his hands, getting the toilet paper all caught up in his fingers.

A piece stuck on his face where he had been drooling. Kevin sputtered and snorted. Lisa laughed even harder. "Kevin has a beard. Like Santa Claus!"

Megan started to laugh too, a tight little laugh from the throat. Then suddenly she stopped laughing and tears started to run down her cheeks.

Lisa looked at her. "What's wrong with you?"

Megan wiped her face with the flat of her hand. "I don't know," she said. "Just leave me alone. Come on, Kevin. I'll clean this up. Lisa, go find something to do."

"Boy, are you weird," Lisa said, stomping out of the room. "I wish Mom was here."

"Me too," Megan called after her sister.

She tried to save some of the paper by gently wrapping it back around the tube, but Kevin started kicking and screeching, shredding the toilet paper and sending bits of it flying all around. Megan sighed and sat on the closed toilet seat. At least he was happy here and she knew where he was. She could clean it up later.

• chapter 6 •

It was late when Mom got home, and Megan was fed up. Lisa rushed to the door before Mom could even get in. "Mom, can we make Christmas cookies tonight? Real Christmas cookies with sprinkles, the cutout kind, and gingerbread too, like at Rebecca's house?"

Mom put a bag of groceries on the counter. "Lisa," she said, "it's awfully late. I haven't even started dinner."

"You promised." Lisa stuck her thumb in her mouth.

Megan glared at her sister. *You are so selfish,* she screamed in her mind.

Mom sighed. "We'll see."

Lisa took her thumb out of her mouth and made

the thumbs-up sign the way Dad always did. "Yes!" she said, ignoring Megan's if-looks-could-kill stare.

Kevin stood in front of Mom and rocked back and forth from one foot to the other.

"How was he?" Mom asked

"Okay." Megan shrugged her shoulders. "We had a little problem with toilet paper in the bathroom, but I cleaned it up." No sense in telling Mom Kevin had been lost, since he really hadn't been.

Lisa began dancing around the kitchen, living room, and dining area and back again, singing "Rudolph, the Red-Nosed Reindeer."

"When are we getting our tree?" she asked as she came around the second time. "Rebecca already has hers."

"Maybe next week," Mom said absentmindedly. She began unpacking the groceries. "Megan, can you set the table?"

"Mom, I have homework."

"I know." Mom sighed and brushed a strand of hair back off her forehead. "Look, just help me get Kevin into his high chair. I'll do the rest."

Megan didn't say anything as she held the chair steady and Mom put Kevin in. She could hear "The 1812 Overture" begin softly as she closed the door to her bedroom. She hoped Lisa would stay out for a while.

Dinner was even worse than it had been on

Wednesday. Just as they finally started eating, Dad walked in. Mom glanced at the clock. "You're awfully late," she said.

"Tom gave me a lift, but he had some stops to make."

"Frank, it's eight o'clock."

"What could I do?" Dad asked. "He was my ride."

"You could have called." Mom stabbed the serving spoon into the mashed potatoes and sat down. No one said anything. Even Kevin seemed to know he should be quiet.

Dad took off his leather work boots and set them by the door. They were caked with cement and mud. He slumped down in his chair and tossed his big old work gloves on the table.

"Frank," Mom said, "not there."

"Yuk. Dad, you're gross." Lisa scrunched up her nose at Dad.

"Oh yeah? It's all good clean dirt," he said, dangling the glove in front of Lisa's nose. He ruffled her hair with the other hand. Lisa sure was annoying, acting so dumb.

Kevin started to bang on his tray with a spoon.

Dad turned toward him. "What's the matter? You want one too?"

Kevin gave Dad his crooked smile and started snorting and then screaming again.

Dad sighed. "So what about the glasses and hearing aid?" he asked Mom. He almost had to shout above Kevin's noise.

Things were so crazy, Megan had forgotten all about Kevin's hearing aid and glasses. The whole reason she'd had to baby-sit in the first place, for Pete's sake. She waited for Mom to answer, hoping it was good news.

"Mr. Johnson said he'd give me a call tomorrow or the next day."

"You mean they'll be ready that soon?" Megan hadn't felt this hopeful all day. Getting Kevin's hearing aid back would solve everything.

"That's just to let me know what they can do." Mom got up to untie Kevin and lifted him to the floor.

"I've got some news too," Dad said, rubbing his forehead and then scratching at a spot of cement on his cheek. He looked at Mom. "The company lost the bid on that big job over in Mercer. So they don't need any masons for a while."

"I thought it was a sure thing."

"Well, I guess it wasn't." Dad got up from the table and leaned with his hands on the back of his chair as if he were holding himself up. "We've got a few small jobs if the weather holds."

"What's 'if the weather holds' mean?" Lisa asked.

Dad took off his heavy denim work jacket and went to the back hall without answering.

"It means if it doesn't change," Megan told her sister. "You can't pour cement if it gets too cold and snows." She felt impatient with her sister. Lisa always had to know everything.

Ever since she could remember, Megan had been having arguments with Dad about the weather in winter. Every time she said she wished it would snow so they could go sledding, Dad would say, "Don't wish that on me. How am I going to keep food on the table?"

Once she'd said, "But I thought you liked the winter for skiing and everything."

"That was a long time ago," Dad had said, looking sad. "Seems like I was a whole different person then."

Megan felt guilty now for wishing it would snow. Snow for Christmas. Snow for the ski trip.

Dad walked back through the kitchen in his long underwear and stocking feet.

"Are you going to eat after your shower?" Mom asked.

"I'm not hungry," Dad said as he went down the hall.

Megan wasn't hungry either.

· chapter 7 ·

Megan's alarm jarred her out of a sound sleep. She hit the OFF button and lay back on her pillow trying to wake up. She felt confused. It seemed as if she had just gone to bed, but the digital clock blinked in electric green, 7:00. Megan closed her eyes.

Kevin must have slept all night. Or at least she hadn't heard anything. That was a good sign, anyway. She sure didn't feel like she'd slept all night, but if she let herself doze off now, she'd be late. She hated starting the day late.

Megan sat up and threw off her quilt. It was freezing. Just the thought of touching the icy floor with her bare feet gave her the chills. She stretched her leg out as far as she could and snagged her slippers with her toes. Grabbing the bucket that held her own soap, toothpaste, washcloth, and tooth-brush, she headed toward the bathroom feeling grumpy.

Megan's mood hadn't improved by the time she finished dressing. Mom was in the kitchen. She was still in her nightgown, and she had dark circles under her eyes. "Megan," she said, "please keep an eye on Kevin. I want to get this load of laundry in before you leave."

Megan poured herself a glass of orange juice and looked at her brother. "It's all your fault," she said out loud.

Kevin stared back at her and blinked as though he were trying to figure something out. His face was still clean and he was still in his bunny-feet pajamas. Megan looked away from her brother, feeling bad. She hadn't meant it, really. How could it be Kevin's fault?

What if he'd understood what she had said? Sometimes he seemed to know what you were talking about.

Suddenly Megan's grumpiness turned into anger. The feeling just surged up inside of her. *I don't care,* she thought. She slammed her empty glass down on the table.

"Thanks, Megan." Mom was back in the kitchen.

Megan chewed on a piece of toast. She felt impatient with her mother, annoyed that she was still in

57

her nightgown, that Kevin had thrown his hearing aid out the window, that Kevin was the way he was. She didn't know why. It was everything. It wasn't fair. Nothing was fair.

"Mom," she said accusingly, "what are you going to do?"

"Do about what?" Mom asked wearily.

Everything, Megan wanted to shout. *You're supposed to be able to fix everything. You're the mother!*

"Mommm," Lisa called from down the hall. "Where's my tights?"

"In the wash," Mom called back.

"Oh, no." Lisa acted as if this were a major tragedy. "I need my pink tights. Mommm!"

"I'm coming," Mom called back as she started down the hall.

Kevin started snorting and banging his head with his hands and making his nasal "Na, na, na" sound.

Megan stood up and slammed her chair into the table. "Shut up, Kevin. Just shut up," she yelled.

Kevin ignored her, and Megan left for school without saying good-bye to anyone.

As soon as she stepped out the door, her spirits lifted. A few tiny snowflakes wandered to the ground and she felt the excitement stir. A sharp wind swept around her and more flakes raced by. Maybe it would be a real storm, she thought. Why hadn't she listened to the radio this morning? A snow day with no school would mean she and Amy could work on their Christmas gifts. Maybe there would even be enough snow to last for Christmas. Then Megan remembered Dad. If it snowed, he couldn't work. She stood still on the sidewalk and concentrated on trying to tell if it was snowing harder, trying to decide if she wanted it to snow or to stop.

She started walking again, and it dawned on her slowly: The snow would do whatever it wanted, and it didn't matter what she, Megan Howard, thought or did or said. It would just happen. It was as if a big weight had been lifted. There was something comforting about not being able to do anything about the weather, and for a few minutes, standing on the curb, waiting for her bus, Megan felt free.

The lighthearted feeling stayed with her as she worked her locker combination. She couldn't wait to see Amy, who had called the night before hysterical about her haircut. "I told the hairdresser just a trim, but my mother called ahead and said she wanted enough off to make it worth the money. I'm practically bald."

Megan smiled at the thought of Amy being bald, like her father. She flipped the lock dial to 27 and pulled. Darn. It didn't open. She must have been off one of the numbers. Or maybe she hadn't started with zero. She hoisted her backpack off her back and rested it on the floor by her feet.

"Hey, Howard. Need some help?" Megan turned before she recognized the voice. There was Scott Wood crossing his eyes at her.

David Morse was at his elbow, pulling on his shirt sleeve. "Come on, Scott," he mumbled. His face was pink to his neck.

Megan felt her own face get warm. "Not from you," she said, but the two boys were already through the stairwell doors. She turned back to her locker, glancing around to see who might have noticed her bright-red cheeks. Everyone in the hall seemed to be busy with friends and lockers.

"Dumb preppy geeks," she said to herself. How could Amy be interested in those kids?

Megan got to first period just as the bell was ringing. She sat in her seat and caught Amy's eye two rows away. Amy pointed to her hair, turned her head around and then back, and made a face. Her hair swung out gently around her head and rested, smooth and shining, on her shoulders, like something from a shampoo commercial. There was hardly any difference in the length. *What's the big deal?* Megan wondered. "I like it," she mouthed to her friend, then lowered her eyes and concentrated on getting her homework out as she caught Mr. Michaels staring at her.

"What do you think?" Amy asked after class.

"About what?"

"Megan!" Amy groaned. "About my hair!"

"I told you. I like it." Megan wasn't sure if Amy wanted to hear that it didn't look any different or not. "I like the way they shaped it."

"See, you don't like it. It's too short, isn't it?"

Megan sighed. "I don't think it looks all that different."

The two girls were moving down the hall, part of the wave of bodies pushing and jostling them. "Well, it feels very different," Amy complained. "It's really traumatic, you know, getting a haircut if you have long straight hair. You're so lucky you don't have to worry about it. Your hair has all that body. Gosh, I wish mine could have just a little."

"Amy! What are you talking about?" Megan stopped by the stairwell and stared at her friend.

"Never mind. Listen. I almost forgot. I've been waiting all morning to tell you. You'll never believe it."

Bringggg! The bell sounded deafeningly right over their heads. Amy stopped talking and waited with an expression of exaggerated annoyance on her face.

"Hurry," Megan said. "I have to go. I'll never make it to my next class before second bell."

"Maybe I should wait until I see you third period. I have to go too."

"Amyyyyy," Megan said, feeling exasperated. "You can't make me wait that long. What is it?"

Amy's eyes lit up. "Okay," she said, dropping her voice to a whisper and talking rapidly. "Kristen called me last night. She's having a boy-girl Christmas party, and you and I are invited." Amy was already walking away and she almost bumped into a boy coming in the opposite direction. "Can you believe it?" Her voice got louder. "I gotta go. See you third period." Amy was out of sight before Megan could react.

. . .

"I'm not going," Megan told Amy for the hundredth time at lunch. Amy had been begging her since third period. They were sitting in their regular place by the windows in the cafeteria because Amy was trying to win Megan's promise that she would go to the party.

"Why?" Amy asked, drawing the question out as if it were a matter of life and death.

"I told you, I don't even know those kids. Kristen just asked me because she knows you. Besides, I thought we agreed boy-girl parties were dumb until eighth or ninth grade."

"That's before I got invited to one. I never thought I'd get invited. Look at it as an important life-broadening experience. You have to go."

"Correction. *You* got invited, and *you* can go. *I* don't have to do anything." Megan folded her arms across her chest and glared at her friend.

"You don't have to get mad." Amy pretended to sulk. "Let's go," she added abruptly, picking up her tray. "I have some homework to finish for math.

"Promise me you'll think about it," Amy persisted as she left for her next class. "David Morse will be there, and . . ." She hesitated.

"And what?" Megan demanded.

"Just . . . you know, and everything. It'll be great. I'll give you one more chance to change your mind. See you later."

"I'll bet all those kids will be there," Megan said to herself. She hadn't bothered trying to tell her friend about seeing David and Scott at her locker. Amy would just think it was thrilling.

Amy had gym next period, and Kristen would be there. They'd probably be all giddy, whispering about the party. Well, so what? Megan had spent plenty of time without a best friend, and she could live without one now if she had to. It was better to be independent anyway.

· chapter 8 ·

Guess I might as well finish up the Christmas stuff by myself, Megan thought as she walked home from the bus stop. She jabbed her toe at an old pop can and sent it rattling across the street. Amy had piano lessons on Fridays, so she couldn't work on the gifts, but time was running out. It seemed as if they hadn't done any work for ages, and Amy acted like she had more important stuff to think about. Like boys and parties.

Kevin was strapped into his high chair with the torn sheet, and "The 1812 Overture" was playing from on top of the refrigerator. Mom peeked through the doorway from the living room and waved. She was on the phone. Megan knew she was trying to find a quieter place to talk and still keep an eye on Kevin.

There was a mess on the high-chair tray that looked like the remains of squished peanut butter and jelly and milk. Kevin started slapping the tray when he saw Megan, and she steered clear of the spray as she went to the refrigerator for an apple.

"Guess that means you're happy to see me even if you don't have your glasses," Megan told her brother. She remembered a little daydream she used to have about Kevin running to greet her when she came home from school, saying something like "Meggy, Meggy."

Kevin smacked the tray and made some snurfing, hiccuping noises. His lightly freckled face was spattered with milk and gunk. "How can you stand it?" Megan asked. She cringed at the thought of having that stuff on her face. It was in his hair again, hardened and crusty. She took a chance and put her face down in front of her brother's. "You little piggy." Laughing, she jumped back as Kevin smacked the tray again. He seemed proud of himself.

What was that? Something else in Kevin's hair. A few specks of something shiny, like glitter. "Hey, what have you been up to today, Kevin? Have you and Mom done some Christmas stuff?" Megan remembered she had been angry with her mother that morning. Now she was glad she hadn't said anything. Her spirits lifted again. The snow flurries hadn't turned into real snow. Dad would be happy, and it looked like Mom was getting some Christmas projects done in spite of Kevin's behavior.

I can finish the cross-stitch for Grandma, Megan thought as she headed toward her room. Mom held up one finger to indicate she'd be done in a minute as Megan brushed by her. Megan waved okay and headed down the hall.

The door to Megan and Lisa's room was open. That was a bad sign, but Megan wasn't prepared for the disaster that greeted her when she entered the bedroom. Right next to her bed was a broken baby-food jar and a puddle with silver glitter floating on it. As Megan got closer, she saw glue and glitter all over her bedspread. Another baby-food jar had leaked on Lisa's bed, leaving a dark wet spot. She picked up the jar, empty of water now, with soggy clumps of glitter stuck to the plastic figure of the angel inside. Two necklaces lay on the floor like snakes, wet and spattered with white glue. Standing on the blue shag rug in the center of the room, Megan looked down and realized she was also standing on two tiny cross-stitch wall hangings, their designs smudged with marker.

Megan drew a quick breath and uttered a short moan. When she was able to think, she knew exactly what had happened and why Kevin had glitter flecks in his hair.

"Mom!" she yelled, running out of the room. "Mom!"

Hot angry tears began to blur her vision before she reached the kitchen. "How could you?" she yelled at her mother. "How could you let him do this?" Megan threw the soggy, discolored cross-stitch work on the floor. There were bits of glitter on it. Then she really began to cry. Her whole body shook.

"Megan, what is it? What happened?" Megan couldn't answer, and Mom left the kitchen and headed down the hall. When she came back, she said, "I didn't know," in a tiny voice and tried to hug Megan. Megan didn't return her hug.

Mom dropped her arms to her sides. "Oh, Megan, I'm so sorry. I was busy trying to get some gifts wrapped so I could bake. The school called and said I had to get Kevin and keep him home until he gets his glasses and hearing aid back. The extras they have aren't working. When I got home, Mr. Johnson from the hearing aid store called with a question before I could get Kevin settled. He must have gone into your room. Megan, please don't cry."

Mom had tears in her eyes, but Megan didn't care. She ran to her room and slammed the door.

Still in her ski jacket, she sat on her bed staring at the mess. Staring without really seeing, Megan made her mind stay blank until slowly she became aware that she was hot and sweaty. She took off her ski jacket and let it fall on the bed where she sat. She pounded the bed with her fist.

Everything was ruined. She'd never have enough time before Christmas to make new gifts. She pounded the bed again. Maybe they *should* send Kevin away. She wished they would. Then they could have a normal Christmas like a normal family with a perfect Christmas tree like Amy had.

Amy! Megan looked at the mess and remembered. Now she'd have to call Amy and explain that her gifts were ruined too. One more thing for her and Amy to argue about.

Megan picked up the whole soggy mess in two fistfuls and threw it into the trash basket under her desk. She'd get it all out of her sight so she could pretend it had never happened. Pretend she had never even started the gifts and forget Kevin had ruined them. The sooner the better.

The only things that seemed to have escaped damage were three of the beaded necklaces. Megan tossed those on the floor in her closet and wiped up the water with a wad of tissues.

Mom knocked on Megan's door and came in. Megan was brushing the glitter and glue off her bedspread, trying to puff it and shake it so the wet spot would dry. She didn't look up.

"Let me help," Mom said. She brushed the glitter into a little pile on the floor with some tissues. "This stuff is a real pain. It sticks to everything." She glanced toward the trash basket and said, "Are all the gifts ruined? I thought maybe I could save some things, clean them up."

"It's okay, Mom," Megan said, raising her head but not looking right at her mother.

"I know you worked hard." Mom paused. "I'm sorry, I should have been more careful. I just left him for a minute and . . . Oh, Megan, I don't know."

Megan had never heard her mother sound so helpless. She felt tears spring to her eyes, but she clenched her fist and held them back. She wanted to stay angry.

Finally, she looked straight at her mother. "Mom, are you going to send Kevin away?" She could ask now because she was angry, but her heart was pounding as if it were going to jump out of her chest.

Mom sat on the bed, looking like a balloon that had lost its air. Guilt stabbed Megan in the chest. *Don't answer. Don't answer,* she said over and over in her mind. *I didn't mean to ask. I don't want to get rid of Kevin.*

"I don't know," Mom finally said. "Dad and I talked about a respite program, but it's so hard to find a family to take someone like Kevin this time of year. I don't know," she said again. "I was hoping his hearing aid and glasses could be repaired soon.

Maybe finding a good residential school for Kevin is the only answer. It would be better for Dad. Better for all of us. I don't want to, but . . ." She didn't finish the sentence, and Megan felt as though Mom were talking to herself now, as if Megan weren't even there.

The respite program was one thing. Different families in the area volunteered to take kids like Kevin for the weekend. It was like baby-sitting for a few days. They'd done that with Kevin sometimes, BHG. A residential school was totally different. It was for all the time.

Mom looked at Megan again and said, "Maybe we'll have some good news about his glasses and hearing aid." She stood up and sighed, then brightened a little. "Look at you. You've got glitter everywhere." She tried to wipe Megan's cheek. Megan pulled away and Mom sighed again. "I'll get the dustpan."

For a minute Megan let herself picture a perfect Christmas tree with Christmas music playing and all her homemade gifts wrapped under the tree with new furniture and clean walls and cookies and new Christmas dresses for her and Lisa. But she couldn't get the feeling to go with it. Instead her stomach felt tight with knots.

Megan waited until after dinner to call Amy with the bad news. It was the one thing she had to do before she could put the whole mess out of her mind, as if it had never happened.

"Oh, no," Amy said. "Not the paperweights and necklaces too? All of them? I knew I should have taken mine home."

Amy was angry, and Megan couldn't blame her. It had been Megan's idea to keep everything at her house. She had thought maybe they could make some wrapping paper too and do their wrapping together.

Megan told Amy about the three necklaces that hadn't been touched. "You can have them," she told her friend. "I'm sorry. I know we don't have time to make everything again, but I still have some glitter and beads and stuff. If you want, I'll bring it to school and maybe you could make some gifts at home." Megan knew it was useless, but that was all she had to offer.

Amy was silent. "Say something," Megan finally said.

"It's not your fault. But you're right, we don't have time to make more gifts. It's too much work. You keep the necklaces. They were your idea. Now we have to go shopping. We can go into town on Monday after school." Amy began to sound excited.

Megan was relieved that her friend was happier, but she felt a little annoyed that Amy could brush away all their plans and hard work with the thought of a shopping trip. "But that's why we made the gifts," Megan reminded Amy. "I need every cent for the ski trip. I can't go shopping."

"Oh, come on. We can go to Dilly's for ice cream. I'll treat. My mom will pick us up."

"I don't know," Megan said.

"You have to. I spent all that time making gifts with you; at least you could come shopping with me."

Megan was startled by the idea that Amy hadn't really wanted to make all those gifts. It was true she didn't need the money. But was she doing it just to be a good friend? "Okay, I'll come," Megan said, "if my mom doesn't need me to baby-sit."

Amy groaned.

"I need the money."

"Okay. I know. Let me know tomorrow. We can go right from school. Tell your mom we have to go," Amy said.

"I will."

"Great, and don't forget to think about the party." Amy hung up before Megan could answer.

Amy was going to bug her about that party until it was over. A party was the last thing Megan wanted to think about. That and shopping. Shopping! If she still wanted to have gifts for her family, that was the only answer. She'd have to spend her ski money, maybe even give up the trip altogether.

• chapter 9 •

"Mom," Lisa said at breakfast on Monday, "I have to have my elf costume for the play by tomorrow. Mrs. Krammer said so. All the other kids already brought theirs on Friday."

"Ohh," Mom groaned. "I forgot." She looked tired again. Kevin had been difficult all weekend. On Saturday he pulled all the buttons off his shirt and almost choked on one.

"I could come home after school instead of shopping with Amy," Megan offered.

Mom smiled. "No thanks. I want you to go ahead. Have a good time. I can't make up for what Kevin did to your things, but at least you can go have some fun after school."

Megan didn't tell her that it wasn't going to be fun. That she was going to have to spend her ski trip money. There was something else that bothered Megan even more. "Mom," she said when Lisa left the kitchen, "I don't want Kevin to go away to a school." She lowered her eyes. "Even if he does ruin my things."

"I know that. I don't either, but maybe it would be for the best."

"We'll get his glasses and hearing aid back and it will all be okay. You said so yourself."

"Megan, Kevin's glasses and hearing aid aren't going to solve our problems. Of course he needs them, and his behavior certainly seems to improve with them."

"Improve!" Megan exploded. "He's totally different."

"Yes, well." Mom smiled a shaky smile. "We don't have to make any decisions yet, and you need to get to school."

. . .

At school, Megan was preoccupied with what Mom had said about Kevin. Maybe it would be good if he got into a respite program again and could go to a qualified volunteer's home for a few hours or for the weekend, but that was very different from sending him away altogether. How could they have Christmas without Kevin? He was one of the family. Even if they had to have a fence around the Christmas tree and listen to "The 1812 Overture" instead of Christmas carols.

Megan was thinking so hard, she almost walked right into David Morse, who was standing outside English class.

"Hi," he said.

Megan felt her face get warm. She lowered her eyes. "Hi," she mumbled. She would have kept going right by David and into the classroom, but a group of kids stood in the way. She leaned against the lockers outside the door, hoping she looked as if she were just waiting for the bell to ring.

"My mom told me Kevin lost his hearing aid and glasses."

Megan looked up. David was standing right in front of her. She smiled automatically and blushed again. "Actually he threw them out the bus window."

David smiled too. "Yeah, Rosemary threw her hearing aid out the third-floor window of our house once. It landed in the roof gutter, only we didn't know it was there until we heard the feedback in my bedroom. I finally figured out where it was."

Megan wanted to ask David if his sister was wild when she didn't have her hearing aid. She didn't say anything.

The second bell rang and the kids in the doorway moved inside. Megan followed them. David was behind her. "Rosemary talks about Kevin all the time," he said. "I think she likes him."

Megan turned abruptly. "Kevin doesn't talk yet." As soon as she said it, she realized Scott Wood had come up next to David. Had he been there all the time, listening to their conversation?

Megan went straight to her seat, which was across the room from where David and Scott sat. Her face was burning again. Why did she always have to blush like that?

Mrs. McNeil was writing on the board. Megan got her books out and tried to concentrate on where she was and what the teacher was writing. Out of the corner of her eye she caught Scott leaning over and whispering to David. They both looked over toward her. Megan lowered her eyes and pretended to read her notes. She tried to remember what she and David had said. She thought he was trying to be nice. But what if he had been joking when he said Rosemary talked about Kevin all the time like he was her boyfriend or something? Megan felt herself turn pink. What a jerk she was. She should never have said anything to David.

Megan got her books together slowly at the end of English class and waited until everyone else was out the door before she left her seat. She did not want to have to see David and Scott, let alone talk to them.

There was no way she was going to that party with those kids. Amy could go if she wanted to, but she'd have to go alone.

...

"I hope you have some homework or something. I told my mom to pick us up at the library," Amy announced as they left school together. It was several blocks to the center of town and the shopping area. The library was a few blocks beyond that.

"Why can't she pick us up at Dilly's like usual?" Dilly's was an ice cream place. Megan and Amy usually went there because they both liked mocha almond chip ice cream and Dilly's had the best mocha almond chip around.

"I have some stuff to do," Amy said briefly.

Megan didn't argue. After all, it was because of Kevin that they were even on this shopping trip, and it was Amy's mom who was picking them up.

"Library's fine with me," Megan said. "You're the one who usually doesn't want to walk that far."

"Oh, come on, twinkle toes, you think you're the only one who can walk forever. Let's get going. My treat at Dilly's." Amy started jogging ahead of Megan. Megan ran after her awkwardly, with her backpack slapping her back.

As they neared the center of town, Megan tried to

get into the Christmas spirit. All the shops were decorated, and some little kids were talking to Santa in front of Randy's Toys and Variety. Megan and Amy stopped to watch. Megan wondered what Kevin would do if he got that close to Santa. Mom and Dad had been planning to bring him this year, but that was before the return to BHG.

Santa gave Megan and Amy each a lollipop and they walked next door to the men's store. Megan helped Amy decide on a leather wallet for her father, and at the jewelry store Amy got a bracelet for her mom. Megan thought if she dipped into her ski trip money she could get something really nice for her parents, but she didn't have a clue about what they wanted. Her father had a wallet, and nice jewelry for Mom was too expensive. As much as she tried not to, she found herself brooding over the fact that the gifts she had planned on were all ruined. And without his glasses and hearing aid Kevin would never learn to make animal sounds in a week. She had been silly to think he would ever be able to do it, anyway.

Megan did buy stick-on earrings for Lisa. Two dollars for ten pairs wouldn't break her budget. But spending the money didn't help her mood. By the time they got to the library, Megan was ready to go home. "Where's your mom going to park?" she asked.

"Oh, she'll come in and get us. Come on, let's go

inside. I told her not to be here until five-thirty, so we have lots of time."

"Lots of time for what? We could do homework at home."

"Just come on." Amy dragged out the words in exasperation as she led the way through the swinging doors of the library.

Megan followed Amy past the magazine section and around the circulation desk. She was beginning to wish she hadn't come or at least that her mom was picking them up. Of course, Mom didn't need an extra job right now, Megan reminded herself.

"There they are." Amy stopped short in front of the young adult section.

Megan almost slammed into her. "There who are?"

Amy put her books down on the nearest table. "Kristen and those kids. Over there."

Megan glanced in the direction of Amy's shrug. Sure enough, there were Kristen and David and Scott and a bunch of their friends. She looked at Amy. "Is that what we're doing here?"

"Kristen said they come to the library sometimes. I thought maybe we'd see them. We should go say hello. Look, there's David."

"You go say hello," Megan said, dumping her books out of her backpack onto the table. "I have homework. I thought you did too."

Megan hadn't told Amy about her conversation

with David and how she thought he and Scott had been talking about Kevin. Amy wouldn't understand. She would have thought it was wonderful that the great David Morse had spoken to her.

"They're waving," Amy said. "We have to go. Be sociable, Megan." Amy headed over toward the table at the far end of the young adult section.

Megan knew she had to follow or everyone would just stare at her. Either way she felt like everyone in the whole library was looking at her.

"Hi!" Kristen said when they reached the table. Megan stood slightly behind Amy. She had never really met Kristen before. "Amy, this is David and Scott. That's Janet, and I think you know Ellen," Kristen continued, pointing to two girls Megan didn't know.

The two boys said, "Hi."

Kristen looked at Megan. "Amy said you're coming to my party."

Megan looked sharply at Amy. Then, becoming aware of the awkward silence, she cleared her throat and mumbled, "I—I'm not sure yet."

No one said anything until finally Scott leaned back in his chair and cocked his head at Megan. "I hear Spiderman has returned," he said, grinning his usual stupid grin.

Megan felt her face turn red to the tips of her ears. She tried to say something, but she didn't know what to say. She couldn't get a word out. Everyone at the table was staring at her. She wanted to disappear right through the floor. At that minute she hated all of them, including Amy and Kevin.

Finally, in a hoarse, barely audible voice, she said to Amy, "I have to go." She knew it sounded stupid. She didn't look at anyone; she just turned around and walked as fast as she could back to where her books were, bumping into the corner of a table. Her sweater caught for a second on the edge of a chair. She stopped to unloop it, then scooped up her books and backpack and jacket and walked toward the door without looking back.

She paused between the inner and outer glass doors to put her jacket on, awkwardly balancing her books and backpack in the crook of one arm and then the other. The shock of icy winter air felt good on her hot face, and Megan took a deep breath. She didn't know where she was going, but she knew she had to get out of the library.

Swoosh. The inner door opened and Amy was standing there with her books and jacket in a bundle in her arms, glaring at Megan. "What's the big idea?" she asked loudly. "Everyone back there wants to know what's wrong. I told them I had to go because my mom is picking us up, but I felt pretty dumb."

"You felt dumb? How do you think I felt when

Scott made that crack about Spiderman? I told you he was a jerk. They're all jerks."

"What's bugging you anyway?" Amy sounded angry.

"You tricked me into coming here. You knew I wouldn't have come if I'd known those kids were here. You said we were going shopping and doing homework. Waiting for your mom!" Megan pushed through the outer door, and Amy followed.

"Look, it's no crime to meet some friends at the library."

Megan felt like crying. She had never had a fight with Amy before, and here they were in front of the library practically screaming at each other.

She sat down heavily on the cement bench by the library door and sighed. "You just don't understand what it's like to have a brother like Kevin. No one understands. People make fun of him."

Amy stood in front of Megan. "Well, maybe I don't understand, but I think you make too big of a deal about it. What about David? What about his sister?"

"What about him? How can he hang out with Scott Wood anyway?" Then Megan had another thought. "He probably told Scott about Spiderman." How *did* Scott know, anyway? Megan had told only one person about that name. She stood up almost nose to nose with Amy. "Amy, did you tell Scott or

Kristen about that? How could you? It wasn't David. He didn't know. I never told him."

"For your information, Megan Howard, I didn't. But even if I did, I don't think it's such a big deal. You said yourself it's kind of funny."

Megan glared at her friend. Amy thought she had all the answers. "I bet you did tell them and you just won't admit it. All you care about is getting in with those kids."

"So I guess I'm a liar too. Well you can go ahead and think whatever you want to." Amy paused, looking past Megan. "Anyway, here's my mother. Let's go. I want to get out of here before they come out." Amy marched toward the curb hunched over her books.

Megan collected her things off the bench. She wished she hadn't planned to get a ride with Amy. If she called Mom now, it would be a nuisance for her to come with Kevin, and Amy's mom would want to know what the problem was. Amy was already getting into the front seat, and Megan supposed she didn't have a choice. She walked briskly toward the car, preparing a fake smile for Mrs. Wilson.

Amy's mom did most of the talking on the ride home. Amy sat up front and answered her mother's questions in short sentences without elaborating. Finally Mrs. Wilson looked at Megan in the rearview mirror. "You two are awfully glum. Or is it just 'shop till you drop' fatigue?"

Megan managed an awkward smile and mumbled, "I guess so."

No one said another word until the car stopped at the bottom of Megan's drive. "Thanks a lot for the ride, Mrs. Wilson," she called, quickly getting out of the car. "See ya," she said over her shoulder without looking at Amy.

Megan could hear the car turn around as she walked to the front door. She bet Amy's mom knew they'd had a fight, but she didn't care. She was just happy to be out of that car.

• chapter 10 •

"Am I glad to see you," Mom said as soon as Megan walked into the kitchen. "How was shopping?"

"Okay," Megan answered, trying to sound happy.

"I hate to ask, but could you take Kevin and try to occupy him for a few minutes?" There were pots and pans and kitchen towels and spoons and plastic containers all over the floor. No damage, just Kevin's usual playthings. Kevin was standing in the middle of the kitchen rocking from one foot to the other, grinding his teeth, and making a motor sound.

"Sure," said Megan. At least he wasn't going to ask questions about her day.

Megan picked her brother up in her arms and he gave her a crooked smile. She was always amazed at how light Kevin was. He was so skinny his arms and legs were practically like sticks, but you didn't notice so much when he had long winter clothes on.

Kevin knocked his chin rhythmically against Megan's shoulder and said, "Ah, ah, ah, ah," playing with the vibrations. She sat down on the couch with Kevin in her lap and patted his back. He rested his head on her shoulder.

Sighing, Megan wished Kevin could be like this more often. How could she even have considered that it might be a good idea to send him away? At times like this she really loved her little brother, and she knew he loved her in his own way. He knew who she was, and he felt different about her than he would about some stranger at a boarding school. Sometimes Megan thought he was easier to love than Lisa, who was always trying to get attention and could talk back. And he was definitely better company than any best friend.

The battered copy of *The Three Little Pigs* lay on the arm of the sofa. Megan leaned over and stretched out to reach it, trying not to disturb Kevin's mood. Maybe right now while he was so calm would be a good time to try a few animal sounds. It was probably useless, but Megan just couldn't give up. It would be more difficult without his hearing aid, but Megan was sure Kevin could hear something without it. His teacher said it was a good sign that he was so intent on lip movements when you spoke to him. Anyway, he liked this book and it was something to do.

Before Megan could settle Kevin in her lap in a comfortable reading position, the front door burst open and Lisa ran in, slamming the door behind her. "Where's Mommy?" she asked. Without stopping for an answer, she headed for the kitchen. Her nose was running and her face was streaked with tears.

"What's the matter?" Megan asked as she put Kevin down on the couch and followed her sister.

"None of your business," Lisa said, and burst into tears.

Mom turned from the stove. "Now what?" she sighed.

Lisa was sobbing and shaking. She could barely get the words out. "Rebecca says she's not allowed at my house because Kevin is too dangerous. Her mom says he acts crazy without his hearing aid and he should be in a special place for sick people like him. She said he could hurt somebody." Lisa took a breath and sobbed again. "And she says his nose is always dirty and somebody could catch a disease from him. And then Carrie said . . ." Lisa was so upset she could hardly finish. "She said she's afraid of Kevin and Kevin is ugly. I told her he isn't, but they both just laughed at me." Lisa threw herself into Mom's arms.

"Some people," Mom said under her breath. Her lips set in a tight line. "They just don't know what they are talking about." She wiped Lisa's face and pushed a soggy strand of hair back out of her eyes.

Lisa pulled herself away from Mom. "I don't have any friends and it's all Kevin's fault. Rebecca says she likes Carrie better than me now." Her eyes filled and she started to cry again.

Megan watched from the kitchen doorway, feeling herself getting angry. "Kevin didn't do anything to you," she burst out. She felt bad as soon as she said it. Megan knew how her sister felt. Before starting junior high school Megan had felt as if she didn't have any friends either. No one ever wanted to come over to her house. She had blamed Kevin too, sometimes. Then she had met Amy and thought things had changed, but they hadn't. Amy was just like the rest of them. Watching Mom hug Lisa and try to make her feel better only made Megan feel worse. Lisa's sobs were contagious and Megan held back her own tears.

Mom wiped Lisa's face with a damp cloth this time. "Try to cheer up a little. I might have some good news about Kevin's hearing aid and glasses."

"Can we get them before Christmas?" Megan

fought to keep an even voice. She stood in the doorway, where she could still see Kevin in the living
room.

"We'll talk about it when Dad gets home. Now
you'd better get back to Kevin. Where is he, anyway?"

"He's okay," Megan said, and went back to where
Kevin was standing in the middle of the floor, rocking back and forth from one foot to the other.

She sat on the couch staring at her brother and let
a thought that she always kept tucked deep inside
come into her mind. What would it be like to have
a normal brother? What would it be like if Kevin
were suddenly okay? Megan knew that kind of
thinking was useless and always made her feel
worse. She sighed and said, "Kevin, do you know
how much trouble you cause?"

At the mention of his name, Kevin stared at
Megan and smiled his crooked smile. It was eerie,
the way Kevin seemed to hear perfectly fine sometimes. Megan had that uncomfortable thought
again. What if Kevin did understand? What if he
knew they were talking about him and it was
always because he was making trouble? He just had
that look. That look as if he knew it all, knew more
than everyone else.

Megan picked up the *Three Little Pigs* book.
"Come on, Kevin, let's read."

89

Kevin began shaking his head and his whole body as he walked over to Megan, making snorting sounds. Spiderman. "Maybe we'll have your glasses and hearing aid soon," Megan told her brother. She crossed her fingers, but there was a weight in her chest.

...

At dinner Kevin banged on his tray and threw his food. Mom had him tied into his high chair, but he rocked until it almost tipped over. She got up to untie him and get him down, saying, "I have some good news." She didn't sound like she had good news, but Megan figured that was because Kevin was making it so difficult to carry on a conversation. "Mr. Johnson called," she continued. "Kevin's aid and glasses will be ready next weekend. He put a rush on them."

"Great," Megan said. That would just make it in time for Christmas.

"How much?" Dad asked.

Mom let Kevin go and sat back in her chair. "That's the bad news. About a thousand dollars."

"Wow," Lisa said.

"Who's going to pay for it?" Dad snapped. Megan wished he would act happy instead of being so grumpy. He was always thinking about money.

"It's the same problem," said Mom. "The state says it's Medical Assistance that should pay for purchase and repairs of hearing aids, but MA doesn't pay enough, so no one accepts it."

Dad frowned and crumpled his napkin. Megan thought he looked sad. "We can't afford a bill like that right now," he said. "Did you tell him we'll have to wait?"

"You mean Kevin can't have his hearing aid and glasses for Christmas even if they're ready?" Megan exclaimed.

"Even if we wait, I don't know how we'll do it," Dad told her. "We haven't finished paying for them yet. Things are pretty slow at the job."

"Kevin needs them now," Megan persisted.

"Of course he does," Dad said. "We're going to have to cut back on some of this Christmas spending. Even so, it will be a while before we can save up the money for repairs. What if he breaks them again before we've even paid for the originals? He'll just have to do without them until we can handle the bills." He turned to Mom. "I'm sorry."

Megan was used to the fact that her family was always on a tight budget. The bills for Kevin's operations seemed to go on forever. Mom couldn't work because she had to be home with Kevin. There were plenty of times Megan couldn't have things she wanted, but she couldn't believe there wasn't money for this. It wasn't like a toy or designer jeans, for Pete's sake.

Mom looked as if she was going to cry. She got up quickly and started clearing the table.

It was quiet for a minute. Megan felt angry. Angry at Dad and Kevin and Mom and Lisa and the hearing aid place and everyone. She felt angry and mean. "This means no Christmas tree, you know," Megan said, looking directly at her sister.

Suddenly Lisa jumped up. "I hate Kevin. Everything is his fault." She started crying. "I hate him."

"It's not his fault!" Megan yelled at her. "You are so dumb. You don't know anything."

"I hate you, too," Lisa cried.

Bang! Dad's fist came down on the table. "Nobody talks like that at our dinner table," he said angrily. He stood up and ran his hand through his dark hair. "Lisa, you go to your room. Megan, you take Kevin to his room while your mother and I clean up."

Megan still felt angry and mean. "It's all Lisa's fault," she told Kevin under her breath. "Come on." She guided her brother toward his room.

Kevin ran helter-skelter down the hall. As soon as he got to his room, he picked up a book and threw it. He scrambled over to the fallen book, picked it up, and threw it again. He picked up a teddy bear in one hand and a rag doll in the other and flung them down, almost knocking himself off balance.

Megan watched her brother. She knew he was just as angry as she was. He could tell when people were upset. He knew a lot of stuff. She felt like throwing things the way Kevin was doing. It wasn't fair. None of it was fair!

Megan caught Kevin in a hug and held tight until she felt the tension in his body slacken. Letting him go slowly, she watched as he picked up his favorite stuffed dog and began making faces at it. Megan giggled in spite of herself. Kevin was making grunting noises, changing his expressions, as if he were having a conversation with the dog. "I know you could make those animal sounds if we worked a little harder," Megan told her brother. "If we had your hearing aid," she added with a sigh.

Kevin was so close to getting his hearing aid and glasses before Christmas. They were going to be ready. It was just because of the money. There had to be a way to get the money. If they had the money, Kevin would get his hearing aid. Mom and Dad would be happy, and Christmas would be perfect.

If Kevin had his hearing aid, it wouldn't matter about any other gifts. They'd go back in time again. Back to the way it had been after Kevin had gotten his hearing aid and glasses. Back to when Mom thought about getting a job and Dad talked about building Megan her own room in the basement. Dad would tell funny stories at the dinner table again and everyone would laugh.

Megan sat on the mattress. She glanced at the bedroom door, making sure it was closed. Then she leaned back and closed her eyes. Money was always the problem. It was the reason she couldn't have her own room and the reason Dad was always upset. Megan thought about her bank account with the three hundred dollars. She had been adding to her savings since school started, and she barely had enough for the ski trip. If she used it for the ski trip, she'd have nothing for Christmas gifts.

Suddenly the answer was clear to Megan. Who cared about the stupid ski trip anyway? She didn't have anyone to go with now. Amy was a traitor. She'd obviously be going with Kristen and David Morse.

Three hundred dollars was almost a third of a thousand. It could be a down payment. With that, Dad could get Kevin's hearing aid and glasses. In time for Christmas. What good was a ski trip if everything else was a mess?

Mom had said the glasses and hearing aid would be ready next weekend. It would be her Christmas present to the whole family. Why hadn't she thought of it before? It was perfect.

"Come on, Kevin," she said, jumping up and folding her brother in a bear hug. "We'll get your glasses and hearing aid for Christmas and everything will be great." Kevin wiggled free and stood staring at Megan with a crooked smile, as if he understood.

• chapter 11 •

Megan wanted to avoid Amy at school the next day, but they had first-period science together. She saw her ex-friend coming down the hall toward her just as she was about to reach the classroom door.

"Hi," Amy said without smiling.

"Hi," Megan said softly. Then she blurted out, "I just thought you should know that I won't be going on the ski trip in January, so you can plan to go with Kristen."

"Oh." Amy looked genuinely shocked and hurt.

For a minute, Megan felt guilty. "I don't have enough money," she stammered. Without looking at Amy again, she went directly to her seat.

Megan sat diagonally behind Amy. All through science she could see Amy's back with the shiny hair that rippled whenever Amy moved. Amy didn't turn around once. By the end of class Megan found herself wishing her friend would turn and flash her a smile and everything would be the same as it used to be.

Megan could pass her a note when Mr. Michaels wasn't looking and Amy would find a reason to turn around, like when they were passing back papers, and mouth an answer. But, Megan reminded herself, Amy was a traitor. She knew how Megan felt about Kevin's nickname but she'd told Scott anyway. Or maybe she'd told Kristen and Kristen had told Scott. Amy was so interested in being in that little clique, Megan guessed she would tell them anything. She could just imagine Amy gossiping in gym class, telling all her secrets and giggling over them.

When science class was over, Amy got up quickly and walked out the door before Megan was even out of her seat. It was just as well, Megan thought as she walked alone to English class. Having a best friend and trusting her was a mistake anyway. She'd learned that the hard way.

"Hey," a voice behind her called. Megan kept walking. She didn't expect anyone to be calling her.

"What happened yesterday?" The voice was right next to her now and Megan turned to see David. "At the library. Why did you leave like that?"

Megan stopped short in the middle of the hall and stared at David. Her mouth was open, but she wasn't sure what to say. Was he trying to bring the subject up again to make another joke? Why couldn't everyone leave her alone? "Because," Megan began more loudly than she meant to.

Kids were passing around her and between her and David. He had to keep moving his head back and forth to keep her in view. "Wait a minute," he said, moving out of the flow toward the lockers. "Come over here." Megan began to feel a little foolish. She moved over, out of the wave of students going to class. Her eyes were on the floor. "Well?" David asked.

"Because," Megan said, more quietly this time, "I don't like people like Scott Wood making remarks about my brother."

"What remarks?" David frowned.

"My brother's name is Kevin. Not Spiderman." Megan spoke curtly, wishing she could end this conversation.

"I don't think Scott meant to make fun of Kevin. He was just trying to make conversation. He said your sister calls Kevin Spiderman all the time. He said she's always talking about the return of Spiderman."

"My sister?" Megan looked up at David. "How does he know about . . . ?" The answer hit Megan before she even finished the question. Of course—Lisa went to school with Scott's sister. Kathy or . . . Carrie. That was it, Carrie. Lisa had mentioned Carrie as one of the kids who were teasing her about Kevin. Figures, Megan thought. Like brother, like sister.

She felt her face flush. "I guess my sister has a big mouth," she said.

"Yeah." David smiled a little. "I used to hate it when my father called Rosemary 'our little Rosebud' in front of my friends." Megan was astonished to notice a slight pink creep up his neck to his cheeks. "Once I even got into a fistfight with a kid because he was teasing me about my sister." He smiled broadly this time, and Megan could see what Amy meant about what a great smile he had. "I hit him and we both got sent to the office for the day."

"Oh no," Megan said but she was only half paying attention to David. Amy! The thought slammed into her. Amy hadn't told those kids. It was Lisa!

"Hey," David said, looking over her shoulder. "We'd better get to class." Megan was startled to see that the hall was empty. Mrs. McNeil was standing at the classroom door ready to close it, looking impatiently at them. Megan walked quickly ahead of David into class.

Sitting in her seat, she glanced over toward David. He was facing straight ahead, getting his homework out of his notebook. Megan saw Scott jab him in the back with a big grin on his face. David didn't turn around.

A wave of embarrassment and guilt flooded over her. She had accused her best friend of being mean and lying.

She thought about what David had said. He knew kids who truly did make fun of his sister. Amy had never made fun of Kevin. Not once. A great relief poured over her at the thought that Amy had not given her secret away.

Another idea crept into Megan's thoughts. David seemed to be able to talk about his sister with anyone. He was blushing, but he could laugh too. Your brother's nickname was a stupid thing to get into a fight over with your best friend, she told herself. How was she going to apologize to Amy?

...

When Megan got to social studies class, there was a note on the door that said their teacher was sick and had had to leave school early. The class was to report to study hall in the auditorium.

Megan chose a seat in the corner by herself. She looked around for Amy and finally found her in the next section, too far away to get her attention. What was she going to say when she finally did see her?

Megan spent most of the study period trying to think of a way to apologize, to make up for the terrible accusation she'd made. Everything she thought of sounded dumb. Megan cringed and slid down in her seat as she pictured trying to talk to Amy. What if Amy just walked away? Megan knew that was what she, Megan, would do if someone had called her a liar.

She went over and over it in her mind—the things Amy liked, the places she liked to go. Maybe she could get her a gift. With what? Ski trip money? The money she was using for Kevin's glasses and hearing aid?

By the end of the period, Megan knew how she could show Amy she wanted to make up. It was the last thing she wanted to do, but she knew it was the best way to show Amy she was sorry. She felt a little better, but she still had to tell Amy.

Unfortunately, Amy wasn't at lunch. She came late to both of their afternoon classes and bolted both times before Megan could get to her. By the end of the day it was obvious that Amy was avoiding her, and Megan was losing her resolve. Maybe it was too late to apologize. Maybe she should forget she'd ever had a best friend, Megan thought. Pretend the whole thing had never happened. The way she'd done with the Christmas gifts they had made.

When she got home from school, Megan found

Mom resting on the couch. Kevin was taking a rare nap. Megan could tell all Christmas preparations had been put on hold. Forget about the Christmas baking—the breakfast dishes were still on the kitchen table.

At least, Megan thought, she had a Christmas surprise for her parents, and it would help the whole family. She wasn't sure how or when she would announce that she was going to help pay for the repairs. She only hoped the glasses and hearing aid would be ready as Mr. Johnson had said they would.

In the meantime, Megan had other things on her mind. Forgetting about a best friend wasn't as easy as forgetting about some ruined craft projects. If she couldn't apologize to Amy in person, she'd have to do it by phone, and she couldn't put it off.

Megan went to her room and waited until she was sure Amy would be home. Then she made herself wait ten more minutes just in case.

She tiptoed quietly back to the kitchen so she wouldn't disturb Kevin or Mom. This phone call had to be private. Lisa would be home in about twenty minutes. It was now or never. Picking up the receiver, Megan hoped Amy wouldn't hang up on her.

She dialed and listened to the ring. Once. Twice. Three rings. Megan knew that if it rang once more without an answer, she would hear the tape of Amy's dad saying, "We cannot come to the phone right now."

Amy's voice came over the line. "Hello, Wilson residence."

"Hi, Amy?" Megan said hesitantly. "This is Megan. Please don't hang up," she added in a rush.

"What do you want?" Amy's voice was flat. Mad.

"I—I want to apologize. I know you didn't tell those kids about Kevin's nickname. David told me that Scott heard it from Lisa. His sister goes to school with her. I'm sorry." Waiting for Amy to say something, Megan could feel her heart pounding in her ears. The phone was heavy in her hand.

"I talked to David a little," she went on. "You were right. He seems pretty nice and I guess I see why you wanted to meet those kids at the library. I know Kevin and my problems aren't your fault." Megan took a breath. "I called to tell you I'll go to the party with you if you still want me to."

Amy didn't say a word.

"Are you still there?" Megan asked.

"Yeah," Amy said finally. She cleared her throat. "I'm sorry too. I should have told you we were going to see those kids, and"—she hesitated—"I shouldn't have gotten mad. You don't have to go to the party. I wasn't going to go if you didn't go. I was too scared, so I gave up the idea."

"You have to go," Megan said. "It's my Christmas gift to you. I can't afford anything else."

"Thanks," Amy said. "I still want to go. I'm glad you called. Really."

"Where were you at lunch, anyway?" Megan asked.

"I stayed in the girls' room. I didn't feel like eating."

"Oh," Megan said. "Me either."

By the time they hung up, Amy was as excited as ever about the party, talking about what they should wear and what they would have to eat.

"I almost forgot," Amy said before hanging up. "We're supposed to bring a grab-bag gift. It can't cost more than five dollars. Girls bring for girls and boys for boys."

"Great," Megan said. "One more thing to spend money on. What are you getting?" She was beginning to sound like Dad, for Pete's sake!

"I'm not sure. I thought maybe earrings. All the girls have pierced ears."

"Gee, Amy, I don't know what kind of stuff those kids like."

"Don't worry, we'll think of something. By the way, does this mean you're going on the ski trip too?" Amy asked hopefully.

"I can't," Megan said. She explained about her Christmas idea for her family.

"Gee, Megan, you shouldn't have to pay for Kevin's things. You don't have enough anyway."

"I want to pay for them," Megan told her friend. She was about to say, "You wouldn't understand," but she didn't. That was the kind of thing that got her into trouble.

Amy persisted. "But how will you get the rest of the money?"

"I don't know yet. I'm still working on it." Megan didn't want to think about that now. She said good-bye and hung up. Now she had to come up with a grab-bag gift before Friday. One she could afford.

• chapter 12 •

Megan solved the grab-bag problem as soon as she woke up the next morning. Luckily, she didn't have to spend a penny. Wading into the chaos of her closet, she pulled out the three bead-and-fabric necklaces that she had thrown in there after Kevin had destroyed the other Christmas projects. She picked out her favorite, one with blue and deep-purple fabric that had a fine gold line in the design. Megan was certain no one else would be bringing a handmade gift, but at least she had something.

When Amy asked her at school what she planned to get, Megan told her she'd already gotten something but that it was a surprise. On Thursday, when Amy showed her the pair of snowman earrings she had bought, Megan still managed to keep her own gift a secret.

On Friday evening, Megan wrapped the necklace, hoping it looked like a five-dollar gift. She opened her bottom drawer, trying to decide what she should wear to a boy-girl Christmas party. The party was supposed to start at seven and last until ten. What were they going to do for three whole hours, for Pete's sake? She had nothing in common with those kids. How would she know what to say to them? Megan had tried to talk Amy into going late, but Amy didn't want to miss a single minute.

Even as she got dressed in her best jeans and sweater, Megan wondered if she could call Amy and tell her she was sick. Of course she couldn't. She had promised Amy she would go. As an apology! She was going and then she'd never have to hang around with any of those kids again.

Anyway, David Morse would be there and at least they had something in common. They could sit around and talk about their handicapped siblings all night. Some party!

One last look in the mirror. Megan loved wearing bulky sweaters, and this one had a rolled turtleneck that she thought was glamorous. She had let her hair dry without using the dryer and it wasn't too frizzy. Maybe Amy was right—a little body wasn't so bad.

Megan picked up the card she had made for Mom and Dad. Both ends folded in so it opened with two flaps in the middle. It had taken all her time after school to paint the card to look like an old-fashioned house. The house had big double doors with a wreath on each one, and when you opened them up you saw the inside of the house, decorated for Christmas, with a dad, a mom, two girls, and a boy wearing glasses and a hearing aid.

On the outside it said, "Merry Christmas with Love." On the inside it said, "This card is to be redeemed for $300 to be used toward the repair of one hearing aid and one pair of glasses in time for Christmas. Love, Megan." Megan had tied a piece of ribbon around the card and made a big red bow in front.

She couldn't wait to give it to her parents, but she wasn't sure when would be the best time. She thought she should probably wait until Mr. Johnson called to say the repairs were finished. But Mom might tell him they couldn't take the glasses and hearing aid now if she didn't know Megan was going to pay for part of the bill. She had considered calling the repair shop to make sure the repairs really would be done in time. Unfortunately, she hadn't had a chance to call without Mom around.

Megan still wasn't sure how she was going to pay the rest of the bill, but she was hoping that maybe it would be less than expected. Given the length of time it had taken her to save three hundred dollars, it would take her forever to earn the rest of the money.

Megan looked at the clock. Forty-five minutes until Amy and her dad came to pick her up. Taking a deep breath, she picked up her grab-bag present and tried to look calm even though her stomach was doing flip-flops as she went down the hall.

"Watch yourself," Dad said as Megan walked into the kitchen. "There's glass everywhere." He had the broom and was sweeping up a pile of glass. Mom was wiping up spilled milk with a cloth and examining the food that was left on the table.

"What happened?" Megan asked.

"Your brother didn't like what we were having for dinner, and he lobbed a spoon at the table. It hit the milk pitcher just right and it exploded," Dad answered. "Spiderman has quite an arm."

"It's a good thing we were almost through eating. I'm afraid there may be glass in this food. I'll have to throw it out. You didn't want to eat, did you, Megan?" Mom asked.

"No, we're having pizza at the party." Megan couldn't imagine how she was going to put a thing into her churning stomach.

Dad straightened up from sweeping under the table. "A party, huh? I wondered why you looked so gorgeous tonight." He kissed Megan on the cheek, acting more like his usual funny self.

"Oh, Dad," Megan groaned.

"It's not fair," Lisa whined. She was slouched

down in her chair with her elbow on the table and her head resting on her arm. "Megan gets to go to a party and eat pizza."

"Come on, sweetie," Mom said. "You and I will start some Christmas decorations if Daddy can keep an eye on Kevin for a while. Then we could decorate our tree, maybe tomorrow."

"Gee, I wish I was staying home," Megan said. "Are we getting the tree tomorrow?"

"Well." Mom hesitated and then said, "Dad and I think it's best if we just use the little artificial one again this year. We can put it up out of Kevin's reach and it won't cost anything."

"Oh." Megan was disappointed. That little tree was only about three feet high and it was old. A few of the branches were missing.

"Mom," Lisa wailed, "you promised, a real tree. A big one."

"I'm sorry, Lisa. That was before Kevin ruined his hearing aid and glasses. I don't have the time or energy, and we really don't have the money. Look what just happened. If we had a big tree with all those ornaments, we'd have to watch Kevin every second."

"Or lock him up," Dad added.

"But what if we could get the hearing aid before Christmas?" Megan said. "I mean, what if they are finished in time?"

"Megan, we already discussed that." Mom sighed. "Besides, there's no guarantee that Kevin's behavior will change overnight."

"Mom, you know it will." Megan argued. "It did before."

"It's not fair," Lisa sobbed. "We should lock Spiderman up."

"Lisa," Megan began, and then stopped. This was the perfect time to give Mom and Dad their gift! "Wait a minute. I have a surprise."

She ran back to her bedroom. The gift would be for Lisa and Kevin too. They'd see. Kevin would change, and they could get a real tree.

She grabbed the card, went back to the kitchen, and handed it to Dad.

"What's this?" he asked,

"Wait," Megan said. "Mom, you come here too."

"I want to see," Lisa said.

"You too, Lisa," Megan told her.

Lisa and Mom stood on either side of Dad. He held the card out and down so everyone could see.

"It's your Christmas gift from me," Megan explained. "Mom, you untie the bow, and Dad, you open the card."

"Megan," Mom said, "it's beautiful, but shouldn't we wait until Christmas?"

"No, go ahead and open it now. You'll see why."

Mom pulled the two ends of the bow, and the ribbon fell away.

"Come on, Dad. Open it." Megan had to keep herself from doing it for them.

"Don't rush me," Dad joked. "I like to savor my Christmas surprises. You put a lot of work into this."

"Open it, Dad. Open it." Now Lisa was excited too.

"Okay." Dad opened both doors with a flourish.

"Let me see. Let me see," Lisa said, stretching up on tiptoes.

Mom and Dad were silent.

"What does it say?" Lisa wanted to know. "That's Kevin and me and our family. What does it say?"

"Megan," Mom began, "this is a lovely idea, but—"

"I know, Mom." Megan didn't let her finish. "It's okay. It's what I want."

"Well, forget it," Dad interrupted. "I'm not having you spend your whole savings on your brother's hearing aid." His lips were tight and his eyes were dark and stern.

Mom put an arm around Megan. "Dad's right," Mom said. "We appreciate the thought, but we want you to enjoy your ski trip. It's our responsibility to take care of Kevin and you and Lisa."

"But it's what I want. It will be perfect, just like we planned, a real Christmas, and Kevin will know what it's all about this year, and—and everything." Megan felt her voice crack with tears.

"Megan," Dad said sharply, "I said no."

"Oh, Megan, don't cry." Mom looked unhappy too. "Please. You'll spoil your face for the party."

"I don't care about the party!" Megan yelled at her mother. The tears were coming now hot and fast. Megan felt something inside her burst. She turned her back toward her family and stamped on the floor. She was so angry, she wanted to hurt something or someone. "I don't care about the party. I just wanted to make a nice Christmas for everybody." She faced her mother. "I think you and Daddy are mean. We have to get Kevin's hearing aid and glasses for Christmas. At least I'm trying. You just want to send him away."

"Megan," Dad's voice boomed again, "don't talk like that to your mother, ever." He started to say more but instead he turned and walked into the living room. A minute later the front door slammed behind him.

"Where's Daddy going?" Lisa asked. Her eyes were wide.

Megan stopped crying. Kevin was banging the tray of his high chair and rocking his head back and forth.

Mom sighed. "He's probably just gone for a walk." She gave Lisa a little hug. "Don't worry."

"I'm sorry, Mom," Megan said quietly. She had to keep herself from crying again. "It's my fault. Dad is really mad at me."

Mom sat in a kitchen chair and looked at the floor. Then she looked up at Megan and Lisa. "I think he's mostly angry about the situation, not at you, Megan. He feels helpless."

Lisa had her thumb in her mouth. She took it out and her eyes filled with tears as she asked, "Will he come back?"

Mom pulled her into her lap and gave her a kiss. "Of course he will."

Megan looked at the floor. She squinted her eyes and concentrated on the tile patterns, forcing them into new designs. She had tried to make everything better and now it was a hundred times worse. Finally she said. "I didn't mean those things. I never meant to say them."

"I know," Mom said. She stood up and hugged Megan. Then she stood back with her hands on Megan's shoulders and looked into her face. "And we do appreciate the thought. Don't worry about your father. He'll be okay. We all get sad and angry sometimes, even Dad. He just needs to get out and think." She squeezed Megan's shoulders and smiled a sad smile. "Now you better get yourself ready for the party."

Megan managed a crooked smile too. "Now I

want to go less than ever. Look at me. Is my face awful? I wish I'd never promised Amy."

"Here, wipe your face with this." Mom handed Megan a cool damp cloth. "You go and have a nice time."

"Are you sure?" Megan asked. The cloth felt good on her stinging eyes.

"Of course." Mom turned to quiet Kevin. She gave Lisa a pat on the head. "By the time you get home, we'll have the makings of a nice little Christmas tree, Charlie Brown style."

Lisa managed a smile. She took her thumb out of her mouth and said, "Hey! Megan won't be here. I can wrap her present. Can't I, Mom?"

"Sure." Mom began struggling to wipe Kevin's face. He was yelling and kicking and dodging attempts to clean him up. Lisa was happy again, dancing around the room singing "Jingle Bells." She glided over to Megan and gave her a hug around the waist. "Don't be sad. Wait till you see what I got for you!"

Megan gave her sister a half smile. "I can't wait." Lisa sure changed gears fast. She could really be a nice kid sometimes.

The table was still a mess. Megan picked up her card, crumpled it into a ball and stuck it in the trash under the sink. Out of sight, out of mind. They could go ahead and get out the little artificial tree

115

and just forget her idea. She watched her mother clear the table.

"We'll leave some of this mess for Dad to clean up," Mom told Lisa cheerfully, "so you and I can get started."

Mom always made Megan feel as if everything would be okay, even if her mind told her it never would be.

· chapter 13 ·

Megan followed Amy into the backseat of the car, her eyes feeling puffy and stiff. "Jingle Bells" was playing on the car radio.

"Hello, Megan," Amy's father said. "I guess you two girls are ready for the big night out." No one seemed to notice that she had been crying.

"Oh, Dad," Amy groaned.

After they were settled and the car began backing down the driveway, Amy grabbed Megan's arm. "I'm so nervous." She wiggled in her seat. "Thanks for coming. It's a great Christmas present. I hope we won't be too early. I mean, I don't want to go late, but what if we're the first ones there?"

Megan could tell Amy really was nervous.

"I love that sweater." Amy babbled on. "Do you

think this blouse is okay?" She opened her jacket to show Megan what she was wearing.

"You look great," Megan assured her friend. It was funny—now that she was on her way, Megan didn't feel that nervous. It seemed kind of silly to worry about a dumb party with some kids she didn't know when Mom and Dad had such big problems. Megan relaxed on the soft car seat in the warmth of the car heater.

Amy broke into her thoughts again. "So, what did you get for a grab-bag gift?"

"I'm not telling," Megan said. "You'll know it when you see it, but you have to promise not to tell it's mine." Megan had her gift in her ski jacket pocket. She hoped she could sneak it into the grab bag without anyone noticing.

"Boy, are you mysterious," Amy said. "I promise, but my fingers are crossed."

Kristen's mother greeted the girls at the door. They introduced themselves, and she led them through the living room. The whole house was decorated for the holidays like something out of a picture book. There were real evergreen garlands wrapped around the stairway banister with tiny gold and silver stars threaded in them. The living room was huge, and there were garlands all around, looped above the windows with big red satin bows. Stockings hung from the mantel, which was decorated with miniature figures of the Nativity, farm animals and angels, and a Santa. They all looked very old and special. The towering Christmas tree was covered with tiny white lights and hundreds of different ornaments. Megan stopped to examine them. No two were the same.

"Your tree is beautiful," Megan blurted out as Kristen came into the living room.

"Oh, thanks," Kristen said as she took their jackets. "A lot of the ornaments are real old. My grandmother brought them over from Sweden a long time ago. This one is my favorite." She pointed to a tiny wooden house, and Megan and Amy bent to look closer. It was magical, with a miniature wreath on the door, and through the windows you could see a Christmas tree all decorated, and Santa Claus, and presents.

"It's so tiny," Amy exclaimed. "And everything is perfect."

"My mom and I made these." Kristin pointed to some tiny quilted calico stars.

"How did you do that?" Megan asked. Maybe she could make some for their tree.

"My mom cut the shapes and sewed them. I helped put them together and quilt them. It's easy. You just need a whole bunch of fabric scraps.

"Here," she added, pointing to a large box under the tree. "Put your grab-bag gift in this." The box was done up in pink and deep rose Christmas paper to look like a big Christmas package. There was another box in blue-green Christmas wrapping. "That's for the boys," Kristen explained.

Megan managed to slip her gift out of her pocket and into the box without the others seeing it.

"Jackets go in here," Kristen said. "Let's go downstairs. The other kids are in the rec room."

Megan lagged behind, taking one more look around the lovely room. There was a candleholder on the coffee table with four lighted candles. Above the candles were three platforms decorated with miniature figures, and the whole thing turned.

Lisa would love to see all this, she thought. *So would Mom.* They could never have anything like it in their house. Kevin would be sure to burn himself, or more likely burn the house down. Mom didn't even let Megan put candles on Kevin's birthday cake.

Megan thought wistfully of the little fake tree her mom and Lisa were going to make decorations for tonight. Even if they had a real tree, it wouldn't be like this. Kristen's tree already had beautifully wrapped packages placed neatly under it. Megan could imagine what Kevin would do to those packages, let alone the ornaments!

Kristen and Amy had already left the room. Megan wasn't anxious to spend three hours with a bunch of stuck-up kids she didn't even know. She lingered for a minute to admire the tree some more.

The doorbell rang suddenly, startling Megan. Should she answer the door? It was sure to be some more party guests, and the idea of greeting people she barely knew in someone else's house was just too awkward. She didn't even know where the basement stairs were.

Kristen's mom hurried toward the door from the hallway, and Megan quietly slipped into the dining room and found her way to the stairs that led down to the basement. Music and voices wafted up the stairwell. Megan was reluctant to make an entrance alone. The only thing she wanted to do less was be caught on the stairway by the next group of guests. She should have gone along with Amy and Kristen instead of stopping to admire the tree.

Kristen came bouncing up the stairs. "Hi, Megan. Didn't I hear the doorbell?"

"Your mom went to get it," Megan said.

"Okay. Go on down. I'll be back in a minute."

Amy met Megan at the bottom of the stairs. "Where have you been? I was about to come look for you. I thought maybe you sneaked out."

"Not a bad idea," Megan whispered loud enough for Amy to hear over the music. "I was looking at the tree."

"Isn't this great?" Amy asked, gazing around the room.

121

The basement was finished, with a tile floor and light paneling on the walls. The lights were dim, and there were more garlands—not real, but pretty—strung with tiny red lights. There was a bar at one end of the room where most of the kids were standing.

"Want some of my Coke?" Amy offered Megan a tall plastic cup.

Megan wasn't thirsty, but she took the cup anyway. "Thanks."

"Come on. We'll get some for you," Amy said, leading the way toward the others. "Scott is telling jokes. He's pretty funny."

Megan stood behind the group of kids who made a half circle around Scott.

"Is that clown still telling blond jokes?" Kristen had come up behind her. "Excuse me." Kristen squeezed past Megan to the center of the group. "Hey, Wood," she said giving a little tug on Scott's short-cropped brown hair. "What color are your roots? I saw a photo of you in first grade. You were a curly blond."

"Ow!" Scott grimaced and patted down his hair. "Only my hairdresser knows for sure." The other kids laughed.

"Hey," he continued, "do you know the one about the blond retard who tried to eat an ice cream cone?"

Before Megan could react, a voice next to her

whispered, "Don't say anything you'll regret." David patted her shoulder. "Just take a deep breath and count to ten."

"Is that what you do?"

"Yeah, I guess."

"I thought you hit people for saying things like that."

"That's when I was less mature. You just have to get to know Scott."

"He's a jerk."

"Scott's not so bad. He gets nervous. It's a big deal to you, but Scott isn't even thinking about what he's saying."

"Saying nothing would be better," Megan suggested.

"Maybe. He does make everyone laugh."

"Not everyone," Megan said, and pressed her lips together in a tight line.

"No, just the rest of us clods. Right?" David said sarcastically.

"What's that supposed to mean?" Megan shot back defensively.

Before David could answer, Kristen stood up in the center of the room. "Okay, everybody. Now that we're all here, we can do the grab bag and then we'll order the pizza."

"I'll help get the boxes," David said, leaving Megan's side.

Megan was glad to have him go. He hadn't

answered her question, and she wasn't sure she wanted him to.

Why couldn't they draw the gifts at the end of the party? Megan wondered nervously. She looked around at all the kids in their designer clothes and name-brand shoes. She never should have brought that necklace. Maybe, Megan thought, she should hide in the bathroom.

Kristen and David were back with the boxes. "We'll go girl, boy, girl, boy," Kristen announced, "one at a time, so we can all see what everyone else picks. No peeking."

Figures, Megan thought, looking around for Amy. She was on the other side of the circle. Megan started to make her way toward her when Kristen said, "Two lines, boys and girls in alphabetical order."

"By first names?" someone asked.

Everyone laughed.

"No, Andy. Last names."

Megan saw Amy giggle and look at Andy. "Too bad," Amy said.

Well, Megan thought, at least Amy was enjoying herself, which was the reason she had come.

The first girl and first boy each drew a gift and moved aside for the next people in line. The next pair didn't wait until the gifts were opened before drawing. A few kids called out when their gifts were drawn, but there didn't seem to be too much concern about who had brought what. Megan had a comforting thought: Maybe she'd pick her own gift. A couple of girls got earrings, and a boy standing next to her opened a music tape. Megan couldn't see which one it was, and she felt too embarrassed to ask.

"Go ahead," Kristen said as Megan stepped up for her turn. "No peeking." Megan reached in and grabbed the first thing she touched. It was small and square. Obviously it wasn't her necklace, but there was no way she could find the necklace without rummaging around in the box. She drew her hand out.

Amy came rushing over to Megan. "What did you get? It looks like jewelry." All the kids were admiring one another's gifts now. Megan struggled with the tape on the box.

"You're right," she told Amy. "It's a necklace."

"Wow, it's nice," Amy said, examining the fine silver chain with a delicate coral pendant dangling from it. "Put it on."

"I'm sure this cost more than five dollars," Megan whispered to her friend, feeling more uncomfortable about her homemade necklace all the time.

"My turn," Amy said as she stepped up to the box. She reached in and pulled out a package. "It's a book. I can tell already." She tore the paper off. "Stephen King!" Amy held the book up for Megan to see. "I'll get nightmares just from the cover."

"Hey, look at this," Kristen called. She had been

last to draw, and there she stood in the center of the group, holding Megan's necklace up to her neck.

"It's beautiful," Janet said. "Are the beads hand painted?"

"No, they're fabric," Amy called out before Megan could stop her. "Megan made it, and it was her own idea. We made a bunch for Christmas. Aren't they neat?"

"I love it," Kristen said to Megan, who was already blushing under everyone's gaze. "Wait until my mom sees this. She works with fabric, and she's always looking for new ideas."

Several of the girls were passing the necklace around and admiring it. The next thing Megan knew, Scott was in the middle of the group with the necklace tied around his neck, wiggling his hips. "Hey, David, isn't this divine?" he gushed, batting his eyelashes in an exaggerated fashion.

"I can tell you from experience, hitting him isn't the answer, in case you were thinking about it." David was standing next to Megan again.

Megan smiled this time in spite of herself. "I guess you're right." She was happy the attention had been drawn away from her and David was still speaking to her.

"Scott always needs an audience. He's kind of corny sometimes, but at least he's harmless. Like I said, he's nervous."

Megan didn't know how to respond. Scott didn't

seem nervous to her. He was up there in front of all those kids acting like a clown.

It was difficult to look amused at Scott's antics, but Megan didn't want David to think she was a total loss. Standing shoulder to shoulder with David, she noticed he was only a little taller than she was. Why couldn't she just talk to him? Finally she blurted out, "So why are you such good friends with him?"

David looked at her as if she were from outer space, and Megan could feel the pink creep across her cheeks.

"Who? Scott?" David looked back at the group. "For one thing, he's one of the only guys I know who's cool with Rosie. Gets right down on the floor with her and everything."

"Really?" Megan asked.

"Yeah. I think he feels more comfortable with her than with normal people." David looked past Megan. "Hi, Amy. Enjoying the show?" He shrugged toward Scott.

Amy giggled. "Sure."

David turned back to the group where Scott was clowning around. Megan felt a poke in the side. It was Amy. Her friend made dreamy eyes and grinned from ear to ear.

"Okay, time for pizza," Kristen announced. "Everybody upstairs."

Amy nudged in next to Megan on the stairway.

David was several steps ahead of them. Amy sighed and whispered. "Don't you think he's nice?" Megan shrugged, looking around to see if anyone had heard. Gosh, why couldn't Amy keep quiet? *Actually,* Megan thought, *David is nice, and he probably thinks I'm a jerk.* That crack about "the rest of us clods" rang in her ears, and she cringed.

• chapter 14 •

Megan surprised herself by eating three pieces of pepperoni pizza. She was just nibbling at the last crust when Kristen came up to her.

"Come on upstairs for a minute, if you're finished. I want to show you something."

Megan took a last gulp of Coke and looked around for Amy. She was sitting on the living room rug talking to Janet and Scott Wood, of all people. She looked as if she was having a great time and wouldn't appreciate it if Megan interrupted to invite her along. "Okay," Megan said to Kristen.

Megan followed her hostess up the stairs and down the hall. She couldn't get over how neat and clean and new the house looked, almost as though no one lived there.

Kristen's bedroom was a little different. Tennis shoes and socks were in the middle of the floor and blue jeans thrown on the bed. But it was a big room with a double bed, and everything matched. The furniture was all the same wood, and the bedspread and wallpaper and rug were all in coordinating colors.

Kristen reached under her bed and pulled out a large flat cardboard box, the kind Megan kept her sweaters in. "Amy told me you like to make your own Christmas gifts," she said. "I made some too."

Megan wondered if Amy had also told Kristen how Kevin had destroyed everything.

"My mom helped me make these pot holders for my grandparents," Kristen went on. "They're quilted. I drew the pictures with fabric marker."

"These are great," Megan said, admiring the designs and the stitching. She'd had no idea Kristen was such a good artist.

"I could show you how to make them," Kristen offered. "Do you think you could show me how to do the necklaces? I'd love to make one for my mom."

"Sure," Megan answered without even thinking. "We have lots of the beads." *As long as we can do it at your house*, she added to herself.

"I made some cross-stitch ornaments," Kristen said, holding up a Santa ornament.

"I like that design," Megan said. "I did some

cross-stitch too. Miniature ones that go real quick."
She hesitated for a minute. "My brother found them
and ruined them."

"Yeah," Kristen sympathized. "My brother gets
into my stuff too. That's why I keep it under my
bed. He's not allowed in my room."

"My brother is multiply handicapped," Megan
blurted out.

"Oh," Kristen said. "Like David's sister. My
mom and David's mom are best friends. We take
care of Rosie a lot. I think she's cute."

Megan wondered if Kristen would think Kevin
was cute. She didn't tell kids about Kevin—only
Amy, and that was after she'd known her for a
month. Kristen just seemed so friendly and easy to
talk to.

"We'd better get back to the party." Kristen said.
"My mom would kill me if she thought I was ignoring the guests." She smiled. "Do you think you
could show me how to make the necklace in time
for Christmas?"

Megan helped to shove the box of gifts back
under the bed. "Sure."

Both girls stood up. Megan looked around as
they were about to leave. "This sure is a nice room."

"Thanks," Kristen said. "Thanks for the necklace
too. I thought you were kind of, well, you know . . ."
Kristen hesitated. "Kind of stuck-up or something.

But you're not," she added quickly. "You're pretty nice." She turned and started down the hall.

Megan was speechless. She followed Kristen down the stairs. Not sure if she'd just been put down or complimented, she was glad she didn't have to respond.

"Kristen," her mom said as soon as they reached the living room, "maybe your guests would like to sing some Christmas carols."

"Okay," Kristen said. "Come on, everyone," she said, taking charge again. "The piano is downstairs."

Megan envied the way her hostess seemed to feel so comfortable with all these kids. She had to admit Kristen was pretty nice, and she'd thought it was Kristen who was stuck-up. Megan followed the group back to the basement. She couldn't help wondering how many other kids thought she, Megan, was stuck-up. Was that what David thought?

The Christmas carols put Megan in more of a Christmas mood than she had been in for days. Even Scott's antics didn't bother her. A couple of the kids could play the piano really well. Amy played "Jingle Bell Rock" and Megan felt a little envious of her friend as her long slender fingers flew across the keys. She knew Amy always got nervous when she had to play in front of people, but Amy seemed to be enjoying it now.

"Do you play the piano?" David asked. He was standing beside her again.

"No."

"Me either," he said.

Megan couldn't think of anything else to say.

Finally David said, "Did Kevin get his hearing aid and glasses back yet?"

"No," Megan stammered. "He didn't. Not yet." Gosh, was that all she could do? Give dumb two-word answers, for Pete's sake? She smiled, but her face felt stiff.

"Do you go to Mr. Johnson for hearing aids and stuff?" David asked.

"Yeah." Another single-word answer! "He's nice," Megan added. "He really seems to like Kevin."

"I know. I used to work for him last summer. Once a week. I emptied his trash and cleaned up. Boy, is his office a mess! His workroom is even worse. Total disorganization. Every week he used to joke about really cleaning up, but I don't think he ever did."

"That must have been fun." Megan began to relax. "Did he give you lollipops?"

David smiled, and Megan noticed he blushed slightly. "No, but I got paid. Twenty-five dollars a week. And, well, we talked a lot about having a sister like Rosie."

"Wow," Megan said. "That's great."

"Yeah, Mr. Johnson is neat."

"Megan, my dad's here," Amy called from the bottom of the stairs. She was already on her way up. Megan was surprised that it was that late. She was even a little sorry the party was over. "I have to go," she told David.

Out on the sidewalk, Amy was bubbling with excitement. "Wasn't that a great party?"

"Yeah, I guess it was okay." Megan was too embarrassed to admit it had been better than she expected.

Suddenly Amy grabbed her in a big hug. "Thanks for coming." She released Megan and danced toward the car. "Ahhh," she sighed before she opened the door. "I think I'm in love. I feel like Cinderella after the ball." She fell into the car across the backseat as if she were in a swoon.

Megan giggled. Amy was a natural comedian. Not like Scott, somehow, who seemed to need an audience, as David said. Megan tried to figure out the difference. Amy didn't take herself seriously. That was it, Megan decided as she got into the car. Amy could laugh at herself, but Scott needed the attention. And what about David? He seemed to really like his sister and he seemed to know a lot about people. No wonder Amy was in love.

...

The front light was on and the door was unlocked. Megan turned to wave to Amy and her father before going inside. She was surprised to see

Dad on the couch. He was lying down with his eyes closed, one arm across his face. "We wish you a Merry Christmas," played softly on the tape player. Megan tried to close the door without making noise, but Dad sat up. He rubbed his hand over his face and looked at his watch. "Just after ten and Cinderella is home."

Megan hung up her jacket. "Where's Mom?"

"She was pretty tired. Kevin fell asleep early and I told her to go to bed." He patted the couch next to him. "Have a seat next to your old man."

Megan sat down a bit stiffly. Dad sighed and put his arm around her. "Listen, Megan, I'm sorry about the way I acted this evening. I didn't mean to get angry at you, and I really appreciate your offer to help out with Kevin. Your mother and I both think you are a very mature and caring person, and we're proud of you. But we don't want you to use your money on things like that. We want you to be able to go on the ski trip."

"But Dad," Megan protested, "I don't care about the ski trip. I just want Kevin to have his hearing aid and glasses and for us to have a nice Christmas and—" She stopped, out of breath, and completed the thought in her head: *And for everyone to be happy.* A big tear rolled down her cheek. She wiped it away before Dad could see it.

Dad squeezed Megan tight for a minute. "I know,"

he said, "but sometimes we can't make everything right, no matter how hard we try." He sighed. "There's so much I want for all my children. Sometimes the holidays make everything seem more difficult. Know what I mean?"

Megan nodded. She liked sitting here on the couch with Dad's arm around her, listening to him talk to her like an adult, but right now she wished she were little again and that she still believed in the magic of Christmas.

"Hey," Dad said suddenly, "I almost forgot. Mom and Lisa had hot chocolate, and they left some for us. I was so busy with your monster of a brother while they made ornaments that I never got mine. What do you say? Shall we heat it up?"

"Sure." Megan jumped up to help.

The small artificial tree stood on top of the refrigerator. It had a popcorn chain wrapped around it and some ornaments made from construction paper and sequins. Megan smiled glumly and thought how much Lisa and Mom would have liked the tree at Kristen's.

Dad caught Megan's gaze. "They saved some for you to help with. It's not such a bad little tree. Your mother is a genius when it comes to working with nothing. We'll put it in the living room for Christmas if I have to guard it from Spiderman myself."

"Oh, Dad." Megan giggled. "Don't be silly."

They sat together at the kitchen table with just the light from over the sink. They were silent for a while and then Megan spoke again. "Dad, we aren't going to send Kevin away, are we?"

Dad was quiet and Megan thought he hadn't heard. Then he said, slowly, "I suppose we have to do what's best for everyone in our family. It's not always easy to know what is best for everyone." Dad looked sad again. All the lines of his face turned down: the lines on his forehead, the lines around his eyes. Even the tiny cleft in his chin looked sad.

Megan concentrated on her hot chocolate, trying to catch the floating marshmallow on her spoon. But the marshmallow had melted, and it mixed into the chocolate in a swirl. Megan blew gently on the hot liquid and sipped the sweet warm foam.

Suddenly Dad made a strange choking sound. Megan looked up quickly. His face was twisted, like one of those modern paintings in the museum with all the parts of the face in the wrong places. It didn't make sense. Then, startled, Megan realized what was happening. Dad was crying. She had never seen her father cry before, and she stared openmouthed as he wiped both eyes with the heels of his hands.

Taking a deep breath, he looked up, smiled awkwardly, and reached out to ruffle Megan's hair.

"Sorry, Meggy. I guess dads aren't supposed to do that."

Megan lowered her eyes and mumbled, "That's okay, Dad." Standing up abruptly, she threw her arms around her father and rested her head on his shoulder. Dad squeezed her back. Megan thought she could stay there forever.

• chapter 15 •

Bright sunshine made a golden patch on the wooden floor when Megan woke up on Saturday. *No snow,* she thought. Maybe at least Dad could feel okay about that.

Megan examined her feelings about last night with Dad reluctantly, the way you might gingerly probe an open wound, not wanting to get too close to the center of it, afraid of how it would feel. Seeing Dad cry had been scary, like a landslide of problems giving way, crashing over Megan and her whole family. Oddly enough, Megan felt calm, closer to her father, and wiser, maybe, more a part of the grown-up world: beyond where she had been before, somehow. She rolled and stretched, testing this new feeling in a different position. A new time zone, she decided, smiling to herself.

There was something else, too. She felt good about last night at the party. Amy was right, Kristen was nice, and Megan had had fun. And David. Talking to David was almost like talking with Amy, only David understood things that Amy didn't. Megan found herself wanting to get to know those kids better. Maybe even Scott.

A door slammed twice; then Lisa began yelling. Megan couldn't make out what it was about. She heard running down the hall and a scuffle outside her door, then Kevin's high-pitched screeching. Megan rolled over and put the pillow over her head.

It was no use trying to drown out the confusion. The muffled strains of "The 1812 Overture" reached her even through the pillow. Sounds from BHG. But this wasn't BHG, even though Kevin didn't have his hearing aid and glasses. Things were different. Megan wasn't the same person she had been at the beginning of the school year. She wasn't even the same as she had been before last night. Usually Megan hated change, but the idea that things never stay the same was exciting too. Nothing stayed the same, and you could never go back to exactly the way things used to be, whether they were good or bad.

Megan threw back her covers and jumped out of bed. This was not BHG anymore, and there was a way to get Kevin his hearing aid and glasses. Before

Christmas! Mom and Dad didn't want Megan to use her ski money, but there was something else she could do. David had given her the idea last night.

She looked at the clock. It was nearly eleven. Mr. Johnson closed his shop early on Saturdays. She'd have to hurry.

Megan thought she heard the phone ring above the music. There it was again. Probably Amy, wanting to talk about the party. She snapped her jeans and pulled on her sweatshirt. "If it's for me, I'm up," she called down the hall.

"It is for you." Lisa bounced into their room while Megan was still tying her sneaker. "And it's a B-O-Y." Lisa's eyebrows shot up.

Megan felt her face get warm. "It is not," she said, feeling annoyed, as she went down the hall. "It must be Amy."

"Mom said so," Lisa called after her, but Megan already had her hand on the receiver. Mom turned down the music and looked at her curiously.

"Hello?" Megan's voice cracked as she spoke into the receiver.

"Hi. This is David."

Megan cleared her throat. "Hi." She felt herself blushing again.

"A bunch of kids are going to the movies this afternoon. I thought you might like to go. We're meeting at the Main Street Cinema."

"I—um—I can't," Megan stammered. Her mouth felt dry.

"Oh." David sounded disappointed.

"I have something I have to do." That sounded dumb. "For Christmas and—and stuff. Anyway, I can't."

"Maybe next time," David said.

"Sure."

Megan hung up and leaned her back against the wall. David Morse had just invited her to the movies! And she'd said no! What if he thought she was stuck-up, like Kristen had said? Why did she have to feel so awkward on the phone, for Pete's sake? Why hadn't she said, "Let me know next time you go"? Or "Let me know how the movie is"? Kristen would have said that. Amy would have. She just never expected . . .

"You okay?" Mom asked with a funny smile.

"Yeah," Megan said. "I have to talk to Amy." She picked up the phone again.

Megan wasn't sure she wanted to go to the movie anyway. She was glad she'd had an excuse. Amy would love to go. Maybe she was going. Gosh, what if she wasn't? What if she wasn't, and she found out that David Morse had called Megan to invite her? Megan put the phone down and went back to her room to brush her hair.

She looked in the mirror absentmindedly as she

142

brushed. So what's the big deal? she thought. A whole bunch of kids were going together. Anyone could have called her. Kristen could have. David called her because he had a sister in Kevin's class. So, Megan wondered, why didn't she feel like calling Amy all of a sudden? Why did life have to be so complicated?

...

Dad was on the couch, watching TV with Lisa. "Dad?" Megan glanced at the clock. "What are you doing home?"

"Job's finished." Dad had his arms crossed over his broad chest. He didn't take his eyes off the screen.

Megan leaned over her father, blocking his view. "Dad, are you really watching Ninja Turtles?"

"Saturday-morning cartoons." He patted Megan on the arm and smiled. "It's okay. Your old man needs to relax once in a while." He smiled up at Megan. "They don't make them like they used to, though." His face was clean and smooth. The sweet soap smell was pleasant. She straightened up and looked at her father stretched out in a clean blue work shirt with his long underwear underneath and thick white socks. He looked cozy, but Megan felt uncomfortable. Dad never lay on the couch in the morning like that. He looked huge. Immovable.

Kevin stood close to the screen, his head cocked, with one eye almost touching the TV. "Kevin, get out of the way," Lisa yelled at her brother.

Dad sat up and tossed the *TV Guide* on the floor. "It's okay, Li-Li, this stuff isn't worth watching anyway." He sighed and rubbed his eyes.

"Dad," Lisa moaned, "he's drooling on it. That's disgusting."

Megan decided it was time to leave. She told Mom she was going to town to do some Christmas errands, which was true.

Outside, she wheeled her bike out of the garage. It was her mom's old bike, an old three-speed. It was about as good as a one-speed, but better than walking to Mr. Johnson's. Megan had to get there before he closed. She stood up on the pedals and pumped hard, pushing thoughts of Dad without work and Amy and the movies and David out of her mind.

It was cold, but she felt good, speeding along with a plan. Memories of last night's party warmed her. How silly that she hadn't wanted to go. If she hadn't gone, she would never have talked to David, and there would have been no hope of getting Kevin's hearing aid and glasses before Christmas.

Megan was glad she wasn't using her ski money for Kevin's glasses and hearing aid. Maybe David was going on the ski trip. She'd have to ask him. Something she could talk about with more than one word! If only Amy didn't have such a crush on David, maybe Megan would feel almost perfect.

Megan turned into the parking lot and pedaled past the row of shops to the one on the end. The neon sign in the window read JOHNSON'S HEARING AID AND EYEGLASS CENTER. Megan chained her bike to a pole in front of the shop.

Mr. Johnson's waiting room was decorated with silver and gold garlands. There was a big artificial tree against one wall, hung with shiny red balls and more sparkly gold garlands. It fit right in with the vinyl furniture.

There wasn't anyone else in the waiting room, and no one was at the little window either. Megan sat down on the edge of a stiff red seat wondering if she should knock on the door when suddenly it opened. There was Mr. Johnson, wearing a red-and-green bow tie and his usual big smile. "Well, hello, Megan. How are you?" He reached out to shake hands. "It's been a while since I've seen you."

"I'm fine, thank you," Megan said.

"Good. And what about that imp of a brother of yours? How is he getting along?"

Megan shrugged and looked at the floor. "Okay, I guess."

"I was hoping he could have his glasses and hearing aid for the holidays," Mr. Johnson went on, "but your mother says it will be a little while."

"Well." Megan cleared her throat and jumped in.

"Actually that's what I came to talk to you about."

A phone rang in one of the rooms in back. "I see. Why don't you come in the back while I get that and then we can talk." He held the door for her. "Have a seat," he said, and disappeared around the corner.

Megan sat on a stool by a workbench. There were some screwdrivers and tiny tools and several machines, one of which Megan recognized as an audiometer from the first time she had been there with Kevin. There were also several headsets and pairs of glasses and cases and hearing aids on the long table.

Megan looked around the room. David was right. Things were pretty messy. There was an old file cabinet with file folders piled on top all this way and that. The trash basket was overflowing and there were lots of books, the big heavy kind that looked important but boring, piled all over.

"Well, now. What can I do for you?" Mr. Johnson pulled up a desk chair and sat down facing Megan.

Megan began the way she had rehearsed, but it came out in a rush. "I know David Morse and he said he used to work for you and I was wondering if you still need someone to help clean and stuff." Megan felt herself blush.

"So you know David. I'm glad you two know each other. Nice young man. His sister is as cute as a button too." He smiled broadly again. "So you think this place needs to be cleaned up?"

Megan smiled, feeling embarrassed. "Well . . ."

"Oh, you don't have to explain." Mr. Johnson looked around him. "I guess I could use a little help now and then. It's getting pretty late to earn some Christmas money, though, isn't it? Or are you looking ahead to the summer already?"

Megan looked straight at Mr. Johnson. "I was hoping to help pay for Kevin's hearing aid and glasses. I could . . ." She hesitated. "I could work for free until they were all paid off, but I was hoping we could get them now. In time for Christmas," Megan finished in a small voice. She was suddenly aware of how silly her idea must sound. It would take forever to pay off that bill.

Mr. Johnson was silent. Not mad. He was thinking with his hands clasped and his two pointer fingers out together.

Megan held her breath. The idea had seemed perfect when she was still in bed this morning. It had to work! She looked around the workroom again. "I could help organize things, even paint a little, really fix it up." Her voice broke the silence, sounding desperate.

Mr. Johnson tapped his lips with his two outstretched fingers, then sighed. "What I really need is someone to redo this whole place. Put in some

bookshelves, a storage area. Give it a little class."
He winked at Megan. "This is a slow time of year.
Good time to have it done. Only problem is, no one
wants a small job. You'd think with times like they
are I could get someone, but these guys all want to
build malls and high-rises." Then he narrowed his
eyes and looked searchingly at Megan. "Have you
talked to your parents about this? It would take a
lot of hours at minimum wage to pay for those
glasses and that hearing aid, Megan."

Megan shook her head, but a new idea had suddenly presented itself. She jumped off her stool.
"Mr. Johnson! My dad is a mason, but he's a carpenter too. He could build bookcases for you. He's
supposed to build some in my room so Kevin can't
get my things. He doesn't have any work right now
and . . ." She stopped, recalling the memory of her
father stretched out on the couch watching cartoons. Having your dad out of work was something
you didn't just blab about to anyone.

Mr. Johnson cleared his throat. "Well, now, the
job I had in mind involves a little more than just
bookcases."

Megan could barely keep from jumping up and
down. "I know, but I'm sure he could do it. After
Kevin got his hearing aid and glasses, Dad talked
about refinishing our basement, maybe making me
my own room down there someday." Megan looked

around the office and workroom. "That's the kind of job you mean, isn't it?"

"I guess it is."

"I know he could do it."

"You're quite a salesperson, aren't you?" Mr. Johnson smiled. "I guess it's worth a try. Did you say your father is home today?"

Megan nodded.

"What do you say we give him a call right now?" Before Megan could answer, Mr. Johnson was around the corner with the phone in his hand, flipping through his address file.

Megan watched from the doorway. She wondered what Mr. Johnson would say if she gave him a big hug. What was Dad going to say when he got on the phone? Megan waited anxiously.

"Hello, Mrs. Howard, this is Sam Johnson." Mom must have answered. "Fine, and you? . . . I'd like to speak to Mr. Howard, if he's there. . . .

"Hello, this is Sam Johnson from the Hearing Aid and Eyeglass Center. Your daughter Megan is here with me now. She tells me you are something of a carpenter."

Megan wondered if Dad was going to be mad. She hoped he wouldn't yell at Mr. Johnson. Maybe she should have spoken to Dad first. Only problem was, she was afraid he wouldn't listen to her. When she had left that morning, she'd had the feeling that

149

moving Dad off that couch was going to be like moving a mountain.

Mr. Johnson was explaining what he wanted. Megan held her breath again. Now he was silent. Dad must be saying a lot, or maybe he was being silent too.

"Good," Mr. Johnson finally said, smiling into the receiver. "I'll be here for another hour. Why don't you bring Kevin along? I'll tell her." He hung up. "Your father is coming over now to take a look at the place. I think he is interested."

This time Megan did give Mr. Johnson a hug. A quick one around the middle. Then she stepped back. "Thank you. Thank you!"

"I should be the one thanking you." Mr. Johnson laughed. "Your dad's going to make more than enough on this job to pay for those repairs, but if you're still interested in part-time work, I could use someone after school for an hour or so once a week. If you are," he added, "you can start right now. Your father said for you to wait here for him."

Megan emptied the trash baskets into the Dumpster in the parking lot out back. Mr. Johnson told her what was in his file cabinet and how to put the files in alphabetical order. She straightened the books and stood them all up between two plain wooden bookends that kept sliding apart until she got them to stand just right.

Dad will be here any minute, Megan thought, looking at the clock for the hundredth time in the last half hour. What was she going to say when he came in? She wished she could disappear before he arrived. She could be at the movies now, for Pete's sake. With David.

• chapter 16 •

The bell to the outer door of the waiting room jingled. Megan followed Mr. Johnson to the front of the shop.

Dad was holding Kevin in his arms. He put him down to shake hands with Mr. Johnson, and before he could even say hello, Kevin headed for the Christmas tree and pulled on the sparkling gold garland. Two red balls smashed on the linoleum floor. Dad grabbed Kevin, who still had hold of the garland, and the whole tree wobbled and then tipped forward. Megan reached out and steadied the tree by the center pole. The branches tangled in her hair and tickled her eyelashes.

"Hold on there. I've got her now," Mr. Johnson said, righting the tree. Megan sat down on the vinyl couch. This was not a good start to Dad's visit.

"I'm sorry about the mess," Dad began as Mr. Johnson brushed the gold garland pieces off his trousers.

Mr. Johnson held up his hand. "Don't say any more about it. I guess Kevin isn't the first small fry to tangle with a Christmas tree. You just make sure he doesn't get cut on those pieces. We'll get it cleaned up." He disappeared into the back room and came back with a broom and dustpan and quickly swept up the shiny red pieces.

"Now," he said directly to Kevin, who was still in Dad's arms, "how's my buddy? Slap me five." Kevin ignored him and started slamming his head back against Dad. Dad put him down on the couch next to Megan. "That's it, Kevin. You watch your sister for a few minutes while your dad and I talk. Looks like you've grown some."

Megan smiled. That was what she liked about Mr. Johnson. He treated Kevin like just another kid. He didn't get nervous or afraid or act uncomfortable. He didn't mind touching Kevin even when Kevin had a dirty nose and was drooling.

"Shall we take a look around?" Mr. Johnson asked Dad.

"Sure," Dad said. He still hadn't said a word to Megan.

"This is what I had in mind," she heard Mr. Johnson begin as they disappeared through the door to the office and workroom.

"So." Megan faced Kevin. "Maybe you'll get your hearing aid and glasses today." Kevin crinkled up his nose and made some snorting sounds. "Then we can work on your animal sounds again," Megan said, half to herself. She took Kevin's hand and held it to the side of her mouth. "Oink, woof, neigh. Remember?" Kevin squirmed and pulled his hand away, giggling like it was all a big joke.

Dad and Mr. Johnson were back in no time. Megan couldn't help staring at the two zip-top plastic bags with red tickets on them that Mr. Johnson was holding. Kevin's glasses were in one, and his hearing aid in the other.

She jumped up off the chair. "You're taking the job?"

Dad nodded and smiled a kind of half smile. "I hear you've got yourself a job too."

Kevin stood up behind Megan, and both she and Dad grabbed for him before he could attack the tree again.

"And we've got something for Kevin too." Mr. Johnson took the glasses and hearing aid out of the bags, bent over, and put them both on Kevin. He made a few adjustments and then stood up. "Just what Santa ordered," he said.

Kevin stood still with his mouth gaping and his eyes open wide. Then he broke into his lopsided grin and started clapping.

Mr. Johnson laughed. "I guess that does make you happy." He grabbed one of Kevin's hands. "Put her there, young man," he said, and shook Kevin's hand up and down in an exaggerated handshake. Kevin laughed and snorted through his nose, looking up at Mr. Johnson with his head tilted to one side. Mr. Johnson dropped his hand, and Kevin did a little dance around in a circle, his whole body wiggling. His Spiderman dance.

"We thank you a lot," Dad said, reaching out to shake hands with Mr. Johnson. "I'll send a formal estimate and be around to start work on the second, if that suits."

Megan helped to put her bike in the trunk and got in the car. Dad didn't start the engine. He glanced sideways at Megan. "I guess I know where you got your stubborn streak from," he said. "I just don't want you always thinking you have to make everything right for everyone all the time. It's an impossible job, Megan. Kevin is never going to be normal, even with glasses and a hearing aid."

Megan bent her head. Was Dad angry at her for getting the job? He didn't have to take it. Of course Kevin would never be normal, she knew that, but what good did it do to say so? Maybe Dad was telling himself.

"I guess the secret is not to give up, even so. I'm glad you don't give up, Megan." Dad reached over and squeezed Megan's hand. "Boy, have we got a Christmas surprise for your mom." He looked back at Kevin in the rearview mirror. "What do you say, Spiderman?"

Megan turned and grinned at her brother. His eyes looked big behind his glasses. One eyelid sagged as if he was winking. The way he tilted his head toward Megan and scrunched up his face, it looked as if he was letting Megan know they shared a secret.

"You mean Mom doesn't know where you were going?" Megan asked Dad as he backed the car out of the parking space.

"Not a clue," Dad said. "I told her I was taking Kevin for a little ride." He glanced at Megan again. "And she surely doesn't know where we're going now."

Megan looked over at her father. "Where's that?"

"You're not the only one who can come up with a surprise," Dad said mysteriously.

"Dad . . ."

"Well, now that Kevin's got his glasses and hearing aid back, I figure he can appreciate a real live Christmas tree."

"Really?" Megan squealed.

"We can't exactly take the biggest tree on the whole lot," Dad said, grinning. "But I expect we'll get a nice one. After all, we both have jobs now. Kevin can help pick it out."

In the backseat Kevin was rocking his head forward and backward at the sound of his name. Megan turned and watched him. Dad was right. Kevin was never going to be normal or even close to it. But something about him had changed. His rocking seemed different, less tense, and he seemed to be doing it for a reason, a reason Megan could understand: They were going to get a Christmas tree, and he was excited.

Even though the tree wasn't that big, getting it into the trunk with Megan's bike was tricky. Megan stood with Kevin and watched as Dad battled the tree into the car. Kevin snickered, shook his head up and down, and slapped his thigh like he thought it was hysterical. Megan laughed too.

When they got home, Megan helped Dad prop the tree up by the front door. They got Kevin to stand in front of it and rang the bell. When Mom opened the door, her mouth dropped open with surprise. Then she smiled and pretended to close the door. "We don't want any," she said.

Kevin began screeching and Lisa ran out the door, nearly knocking Dad over with a hug. "Daddy," she squealed, "where did you get it?"

Before anyone could answer, Lisa grabbed Megan in a hug too. "You're my best sister."

"I'm your only sister," Megan reminded her laughing.

They brought the tree in and Dad explained to Mom about the job with Mr. Johnson.

. . .

"Megan," Mom said after they had the tree up in the stand, "there's been so much excitement around here, I almost forgot to tell you. Amy called three times while you were out. I told her I'd have you call as soon as you got in. It must be important. Also a David called. He said to tell you that no one else could go to the movie after all, so they'll make it another time. He'll call back."

Megan continued stringing popcorn. Kevin was playing with a pile of popped corn on the floor. Lisa was dancing around the living room and kitchen singing Christmas carols. Dad had gone out to get more lights for the tree. Megan sighed. It was the perfect Christmas scene. She was afraid if she called Amy, it would all disappear. David had called twice in one day, and instead of feeling good about it, Megan felt guilty. If she talked to Amy, she'd have to tell her.

Mom looked at Megan, cocking her head. "Well, aren't you going to call Amy?"

"Later," Megan told her. And then because Mom looked puzzled she added, "I want to get this chain done before Dad gets back with the lights."

Practically before she finished speaking, the phone rang. "I'll get it," Lisa called from the kitchen. A pause. "It's for you, Megan, and it's not a boy. It's just Amy."

Megan cringed as she got up to take the call. She was sure Amy had heard her sister.

Lisa was standing holding the receiver. Megan took the phone from her and covered the mouthpiece with her hand. "Pleeease go help Mom with the popcorn." To her surprise, Lisa skipped away. Megan said hello.

"It's about time you got home. Where were you? I've been calling all day." Amy didn't give Megan a chance to answer. "I talked to Kristen this morning, and guess what she told me."

Megan waited for Amy to tell her.

"Megan, are you there?"

"Sure."

"Well, are you okay? Say something."

"Sure I'm okay. Guess what—we got a Christmas tree today, a real one, and Kevin got his glasses and hearing aid, and we're decorating the tree now."

"Megan, that's great! Now listen." Amy acted as though Megan's news was unimportant. Megan was about to point that out when she heard her friend say, "I talked to Kristen this morning, and she told me that David Morse likes you."

Megan felt her face get warm down to her neck. She was blushing even though no one was around, for Pete's sake. "So?" she asked, surprised to hear her voice sounding defensive.

"What's that supposed to mean? Didn't you hear me?"

"I mean, well, he called me today to go to the movies, and I thought you'd be mad or—or something," Megan blurted out.

"Yeah, well, David's too short. I measured. And . . ." Amy hesitated. "I like someone else."

"You do?" Megan asked.

"Don't you want to know who?"

"Sure."

"Scott. Scott Wood."

"You do?" Megan asked again. Amy didn't like David! But Scott Wood? Megan wasn't exactly sure what to say.

"You're not mad, are you? I mean, I know you can't stand him, but Megan, he's really funny, and you won't believe it, but he's really shy when he's not in front of a big group, and I wasn't going to tell you, but well, you're my best friend."

Megan started to giggle.

"What's so funny?" Amy sounded annoyed, but Megan couldn't help it. "Megan, if you can't be serious, I'm going to hang up," Amy said, and then she started laughing too.

When they finally stopped laughing, Megan said, "I'm not mad," and Amy said, "Me either," and they started laughing again.

. . .

At dinner that night, Kevin ate messily, using his fingers and drooling and making lots of noise, but without spitting or kicking and yelling. Dad shook his head, but he was smiling. "Kevin," he said, reaching over to touch Kevin on the shoulder, "maybe your name should be Piggy instead of Spiderman."

Kevin twisted around and shrugged his shoulder to get Dad's hand off. He scrunched up his face and went back to eating his hamburger pieces.

When he was finished, Mom let him get down and play around on the floor. He crawled under the table, and Dad tickled him with his foot. They could hear Kevin sputter and giggle.

Dad peeked under the table. "Kevin, are you a little doggie under there?" he asked. "Here doggie, nice doggie." Dad put his hand down to pet Kevin. When he sat up again he said, "Maybe that's what we need around here, a puppy."

"Oh, Frank, don't be crazy," said Mom. "That's the last thing we need."

Dad smiled. "Just kidding."

"Oh shucks," Lisa said.

"Well, at least we have to wait until Kevin is a little older. Maybe by next Christmas." Mom sure seemed relaxed! She looked pretty too. Her hair was combed and shiny and the dark circles were gone from under her eyes.

"Watch out," Dad told her. "Better not make any promises you won't want to keep." He winked, and Megan could tell he was happy. Dad had been talking about getting a dog for years.

A few minutes later Kevin came out from under the table and stood in front of Dad. He rocked back and forth from one foot to the other, making his crooked grin.

He pointed to himself. "Woof, woof," he said loud and clear. "Woof, woof." He clapped his hands and laughed.

Megan stared at her brother. She could hardly believe her ears. Before anyone could say a word, Kevin did something even more unbelievable. He pointed at Dad. "Oink, oink. Oink, oink," he said as clearly as Megan would say it herself. Then he doubled over with his snickering laughter.

For a long moment no one at the table spoke. Then Lisa shouted, "Kevin is calling Daddy a pig!" She started to laugh, and then Mom started too. Megan could see she was trying not to but it just came bursting out. Kevin looked at Mom and then drew himself up as if he were proud of what he had done.

Megan looked at Dad, who was staring at Kevin with his mouth open, and started laughing herself.

"Oink, oink," Kevin kept saying, getting sillier and sillier, snickering and oinking until he was practically choking. Then Dad, too, started to laugh.

Hot tears rolled down Megan's cheeks. She laughed until her stomach ached and still she could barely stop. Finally she took a deep breath and tried to sit calmly. Wiping her cheeks, she noticed that Dad had tears in his eyes.

Kevin stopped laughing and looked at everyone as though he were being very serious. "Oink, oink," he said one more time.

Lisa hiccuped. "Megan taught him that," she said breathlessly. "She's been working on it all the time."

Dad pulled Kevin over and wrapped him into a hug.

Mom got up and hugged Megan. "I have to admit, sometimes I thought he couldn't do it," she said.

Dad put Kevin on his knee. "My own son calling me a pig. Is that what you taught him, Megan?"

Lisa climbed into Dad's lap too.

Megan giggled. "It was supposed to be a Christmas present. I guess Kevin couldn't wait."

Kevin wagged his head and wiggled all over at the sound of his name.

Mom's cheeks were rosy from all the laughing. Her eyes were shiny. She stretched her arms around Dad and Lisa and Kevin. "It's the best Christmas present ever," she said, smiling at Megan.

Megan looked at her family. They made a perfect picture. Not perfect like Amy's Christmas tree or Kristen's room, where everything matched. It was the design her family made that was perfect, off center but balanced.

Kevin and all their problems added to the picture, like the big uneven stitches in a handmade gift that Mom always said made it special.

Megan wished everything could stay the way it was that very minute, but she knew it wouldn't, and she, Megan, couldn't do anything about it. Dad was right when he said she couldn't make everything right for everyone all the time. Things happened, and sometimes they happened better than she could have planned them. Things like being friends with Kristen and making ornaments with her. Getting to know David and finding out he wasn't a jerk. She had a job and enough money to go on the ski trip and it was going to be a perfect Christmas this year.

In fact, it already was.

• About the Author •

Karen Lynn Williams received a B.A. in Speech Pathology from the University of Connecticut and an M.S. in Deaf Education from Southern Connecticut State University. *A Real Christmas This Year* is based in part on her experiences as a teacher of hearing-impaired children. Ms. Williams now writes full time. She and her husband, a physician, have four children. They have lived in Africa and Haiti and now make their home in Pittsburgh, Pennsylvania.